BBC CHILDREN IN NEED

STORY
COLLECTION

First published in 2002 by BBC Worldwide Limited
Woodlands, 80 Wood Lane, London W12 0TT
2 4 6 8 10 9 7 5 3 1

ISBN 0 563 53240 8
Printed and bound in England

BBC CHILDREN IN NEED
STORY
COLLECTION

Foreword

BBC Children in Need helps disadvantaged children and young people in the UK aged 18 and under, including those affected by homelessness, neglect, abuse, poverty, illness, disability and addiction. This BBC Children in Need Story Collection has been produced to help raise funds for those children. It is fitting for BBC Children in Need to have its own book, because books bring pleasure to children of all ages and backgrounds.

The authors generously submitted their stories, and the illustrator of *How I Stole Your Brain* his illustrations, and we thank them for a collection that is magical, thought-provoking, sensitive and, sometimes, downright silly!

We hope that the book becomes a favourite, for years to come.

To receive a Supporter Pack with ideas on how to fundraise for BBC Children in Need please call 0845 607 3333 or email pudsey@bbc.co.uk.

Contents

Problems
Jacqueline Wilson

Miss Drummond drones on and on about these awful Maths problems. I can't understand Maths even if I concentrate until the steam comes out of my ears. Besides, I've got other things on my mind. I doodle on the back of my Maths book, write my name all sorts of fancy ways and surround each posh squiggly signature with elaborately entwined flowers. Then I write down Damian Chatham. He's this boy I like in our class. He's not my boyfriend. I wish! Damian's not the most good-looking boy and he's not the cleverest and he's not the best at sports – but he's funny and kind and I like him lots, though I'm too shy to let on to anyone, apart from my friend Lucy.

I don't know if Damian likes me or not. He said he liked my long hair once. And another time when I dropped the ball in Rounders and everyone groaned he said quietly, 'Don't worry, Nicola.' But that doesn't really mean anything. He's nice to everyone. He's nice to my friend Lucy. She's nuts about him, too.

There's a little poke in my back. I turn around. Lucy passes me a note, keeping a wary eye on Miss Drummond. I have a peek under my desk.

Dear Nicola – Isn't this BORING!!! Do you have a clue what she's on about? Jenny and Mags and I are going down the Rec near my house after school. Want to come? Love Lucy. P.S. Damian and his mates often hang out there.

I read Lucy's note. I read it again. I read the last line over and over. I want to go down to the Rec with Lucy and Jenny and Mags – and maybe Damian! Soooo much. But I can't.

Dear Lucy – I write – Sorry, I can't make it after school. Don't you dare get off with Damian yourself! I haven't got a clue about the Maths problems either. Old Drummond could be talking some obscure Tuareg dialect for all I know –

Lucy never gets my note because Miss Drummond stops her long, involved Mathematical discourse and sees me scribbling. She asks me what I'm writing. I say, 'Nothing, Miss Drummond.' She sighs, beckons, and holds out her hand. I have to give her the note. She raises her eyebrows at the Old Drummond Tuareg bit. I hold my breath.

I'm terrified she'll give me a detention. I have to get back home for Mum. They know a bit about her at school, but they don't know how bad things are now. They still think Dad's around anyway. We can't tell them in case they have to report it.

It's almost a relief when Miss Drummond sets me extra Maths homework instead. I won't be able to do it, of course. I'll have to suck up to Clever Clogs Chrissie and bribe her with the Kit Kat from my packed lunch to see if she'll do the Maths problems for me.

"Sorry you got caught, Nicks," says Lucy, when the bell goes. "You coming to the Rec, then?"

"I can't, Lucy."

"You *can*. Look, I tell you, I heard Damian chatting to Jack and Liam and Little Pete. They're planning to play footie there."

"You know I have to do the shopping for my Mum."

"Yeah, but you could do that after."

"I can't be late for her."

Lucy sighs. She knows about my Mum and me. I've sworn her to secrecy. But she doesn't understand.

"You've got to have some life of your *own*, Nicola," she says. Like it's a choice I can make.

Lucy's my best ever friend but sometimes I feel like we're poles apart. She's at the North Pole spinning under the stars with Jenny and Mags and Jack and Liam and Little Pete and my Damian – and I'm down at the South Pole all by myself, unable to get hold of my own life.

I rush off without even saying goodbye properly. I don't want Lucy to see I've got tears in my eyes. I blink furiously and hurry down to Tesco's and buy all the food and stuff.

Then I have to go to Boots and stand at the counter with these big packs of incontinence pads. I should be used to it by now but I still go bright red, scared that people will think they're for *me*, though I know no one can *help* being incontinent and it's nothing to be ashamed of.

I peer just for a moment in *Tammy* but I haven't got time for a proper look and there's no point anyway. We haven't got any spare cash.

Then I lumber everything home. There's no bus that goes near our flats and taxis are out of the question. My arms ache and I feel hot and tired and fed up. I can't help thinking about Lucy and the girls down the Rec, sitting on the swings, giggling away, watching Damian and the others kicking a football about. Then the ball gets kicked near them, Lucy catches it, Damian comes running over, they have a little laugh together, Lucy tosses her lovely shiny hair out of her eyes, Damian stares at her, smiles...

It's as if it is actually happening in front of me. It's not *fair*.

But it's stupid getting worked up about it. 'Stupid, stupid, stupid,' I hiss to myself as I go into our estate. I keep my eyes down and just nod quickly whenever anyone says 'hello'. We can't have anyone getting too friendly and coming around. If they saw how bad Mum is now they'd maybe start interfering.

I have to trail up three flights of stairs because the lifts are broken again. Just as well we don't live right up on the fifteenth floor. Still, I don't suppose it makes much difference to Mum.

I stop in front of our front door. I wipe my eyes. I breathe deeply. I stretch my lips into a great big smile. Then I let myself in.

"Cooee, Mum," I go, as I always do.

There's a little pause. My heart thumps – but then, faintly, "Cooee, Nicky," comes from the living room.

I dump the shopping in the hall and go and see her. She's got her bag open and a tissue in her hand. Maybe she was having a little weep herself? Her eyes look red. But she's got her own smile firmly fixed in place.

"Hi there, my best girl," she says.

"Wotcha, my best Mum," I say. "Cup of tea?"

"Yes, please," she says, but her smile slips. "Oh, Nicky, if only I could have a cup of tea waiting for *you*, like a proper Mum."

"Oh, so are you an *improper* Mum?" I say quickly, taking her lunchtime tray. She's tipped her cup over but she's started using one of those ones with a lid and spout so it doesn't spill. She's got sandwich crumbs all down her front though. She sees me looking and tries to brush them away but her hands are so feeble nowadays they're not much use. She tries so hard to keep herself nice but on a bad day she can't even brush her hair or do her own make-up. Some days she doesn't feel like it anyway. She just says 'What's the point?' and sits and stares into space. Those are the scariest days.

My Mum has got this progressive illness. It means she can't get better. She can only get worse. She can't manage more than a couple of steps now. She can't lift anything with her hands. She can't get to the loo in time. She can't even bathe herself now.

11

Mum hasn't always been like this. She used to be fit and healthy and strong. Stronger than most Mums. I remember one day when I was little and we were on holiday at the seaside. Mum and I were paddling together, holding hands, jumping waves – but then a big wave came and I slipped and went under. I got scared but Mum scooped me up and whirled me round and round so that my toes skimmed the water and it was just like I was flying. We ran races along the sands later to get warm and Mum always beat me. She could even beat my Dad.

He cleared off last year. He was OK when Mum was first diagnosed. She was just a bit clumsy and fell over every now and then. Dad helped her and said he was sure she'd get better in time. But she didn't get better, she gradually got worse. Dad cried the first time she had to use a wheelchair. He said it made him feel so bad. How did he think it made Mum feel?

Dad got more and more depressed and started staying out late. He said it was because he couldn't bear to watch Mum suffer. But he'd started seeing this woman at his work. He lives with her now. He still sends us money – well, most of the time. But he hardly ever comes to see us. Still, we manage fine without him.

Well, we did. But it's getting harder and harder now. Mum's getting worse. She won't see the doctor anymore. She says there's no point because he can't cure her. Mum won't see anyone in case they tell on us. If people find out that Dad's gone for good and I'm the only one looking after Mum then they might split us up. Mum would end up in a Home and I'd end up in Care.

We couldn't bear that. We've got to stay together no matter what. So it's like I've taken over. I'm like the Mum and she's like my little baby. I do everything for her. I don't *want* to. I get fed up lots of times. But what else can I do?

I know that one day Mum will get so bad she won't be able to be left. I don't know what I'm going to do then. I've thought about dashing home at lunchtime, bunking off school altogether – but then they'd investigate.

It's like one of Miss Drummond's Maths problems. I can't seem to come up with any answer. And sometimes when Lucy goes on and on about life being so unfair because her Mum won't buy her this new leather jacket or her Dad won't let her go to a disco I just stare at her and think, if only I had *your* problems, Lucy. But I don't go on at her. Lucy's my friend. Even if she does get off with Damian.

I think about them as I make Mum's tea and sort her out. I think about them as Mum and I watch telly while we eat. I think about them as I do the dishes and put the sheets in the washing machine and start on yesterday's ironing.

Then the phone rings.

It'll be Lucy. All set to show off. Telling me about her and Damian.

"Nicky? It won't be for me," Mum calls.

"Oh, I'm busy, Mum," I yell from the kitchen. "It doesn't matter. Just let it ring."

It rings and rings. I hear Mum grunt as she drags herself sideways, reaching out for it with one shaky hand.

"Don't, Mum!" I shout – but she's already answering.

"Nicky?" Mum calls. "Someone to speak to you."

I sigh. I close my eyes. I practise saying "Good for you, Lucy. Sure, it's cool with me. I hope you and Damian are very happy."

But it's not Lucy. When I trudge into the living room Mum mouths at me 'It's a boy!' She grins at my shocked face.

My hands are shaking as I snatch the phone.

"Hi, Nicola. It's me, Damian."

I swallow. I say 'hi' back in such a silly squeak he doesn't hear me.

"Nicola?"

"Hello Damian."

"I've just been at the Rec with my mates."

"Oh. Yeah?"

"And Lucy and them were there, too."

Oh no, *he's* going to tell me that they've made friends.

13

"Right," I say tensely.

"I hoped you might be there, too."

"Oh. No. I – I had things to do."

"Yes, Lucy said. I asked her for your phone number. I hope that's all right?"

"Mmm." My heart is beating so fast I'm sure he can hear it.

"Lucy said your Mum's not well and you have to do the shopping and that?"

"Yes."

"Well, maybe – maybe I could help you with the shopping sometimes?"

"With your mates?"

"No! Just you and me. I could help you carry the bags. If you'd like?"

"Oh. Well." Thank goodness I've just stocked up at Boots! But I suppose it wouldn't matter if he came round Tesco's with me. In fact, it would be wonderful.

Mum is looking at me, nodding determinedly.

"Say YES!" she mouths.

"OK then. Yes. If you're sure you wouldn't mind."

"I'd like to. OK? Well, see you at school tomorrow and we'll maybe go shopping after."

"Yes. Damian? Thanks for phoning."

I put the phone down, dazed. Mum's smile is real this time, from one ear to the other.

"Oh Nicky, he sounds so sweet. Now look, after you go shopping together go to McDonald's, right?"

"But Mum, I can't. You'll be waiting."

"And I can wait a bit longer. I just want you to have a little bit of fun, sweetheart. Goodness knows, you deserve it. You have to do so much for me."

"And I always will, Mum," I say.

I give her a big hug and just at this moment I'm so happy I feel strong enough to scoop her up out of danger and whirl her round and round and keep her flying forever.

Old Dog, New Tricks
Allan Ahlberg

I was a happy old dog – eating my biscuits, lying in the sun …until the puppy came. A comfortable old dog – drinking from my bowl, dozing in my basket…until that puppy.

That puppy – what a pest! Why ever would anybody *want* one? All the noise – all the racing around – all the mess. And no manners at all. *My* biscuits – *my* basket – *my* bowl – just as though they were his very own.

I was a lucky old dog – a family that made a fuss of me, my own special blanket in the car, until that little…*puppy* showed up. After that my life was never the same. Morning, noon and night, he simply took over. And my family let him do it. I was never jealous, of course, though it seemed to me they were more *his* family now. I was just that old dog in the corner.

The Mr and the Mrs were forever picking him up and talking to him. The children raced home from school to play with him. Even the baby's little eyes lit up when that small bag of fur came skidding into the room. And me? I could have been a piece of the furniture. I could have been a rug.

The worst thing was the yapping...from half-past five in the morning. A good night's sleep in that house was a thing of the past. There again, really the *worst* thing, absolutely the worst, was the licking. I would wake up sometimes and there he'd be, *licking my ear*. Yuk.

Then all of a sudden one morning – bliss. No licking, no yapping...no puppy.

Don't ask me how he got out; I couldn't tell you, but he did. Anyway, once my family realized he was gone, they were frantic, rushing round the house and garden then disappearing in all directions looking for him. The Mr bouncing the baby down the road in his pushchair, the Mrs still in her slippers, the children...wild.

And me? It was no business of mine. I returned to the peace and quiet of my basket and let them get on with it.

It was a warm morning and likely to become a hot day. I could have done with a cool fresh bowl of water. No chance of that. Anyway, by and by back they all came: breathless, sweating, unhappy-looking...and the baby was crying. No puppy.

They sat around in the kitchen. The Mrs made a phone call. The children kept darting out into the garden. The baby kept crying. I stood next to my bowl, trying to catch somebody's attention. Hopeless.

All the doors of the house were open wide. A breeze was blowing, and *on* the breeze...I padded out of the kitchen (what was I *doing*?) and across the hall. That pest of a puppy ...I could smell him.

As you will know, all creatures have their own particular smell and this puppy was no exception. Actually, puppies I've noticed have an even more distinctive smell (like all babies perhaps). It's a bit like…I don't know, like fresh-baked bread or something. Anyway, it was *his* smell and I could smell it. I sometimes think we dogs could live in this world blindfold.

His trail began not on the polished kitchen floor or the hall tiles but on the back doormat. He had kicked his stubby little legs there, dragged his baby claws in the coarse fibres. I set off down the road trailing him. (Don't ask me why.) Luckily he had stayed mostly on the grass verge. The pads of his tiny feet had left their traces in the still damp grass. Also, of course, he had left his mark from time to time, as we dogs do, against various posts and fences. It all helped.

I passed the postman – another dog of my acquaintance – a bag of crisps that somebody had dropped (cheese and onion, not one of my favourites). I kept going.

Traffic lights – traffic – car fumes (I almost lost him then) – crowds – noise. (What *was* I doing?)

Eventually, the trail of this runaway pup turned in at the park gates…and there he was. I could see him. I could *hear* him. He was down by the pond after the ducks. He was yapping, they were quacking, some old lady was trying to shoo him away.

I gave him a bark and to my surprise really he left the ducks and came scampering up. He was half-soaked, of course, and shook himself, *of course*, all over me. Then, would you believe it, he was back in the pond again and some big old swan was steaming up looking irate. (And why not?) I was forced to wade in after him – get between him and this huge mad bird. They can break a dog's leg with their wings, you know.

Next thing, we're away from there, out on the grass. I'm as soaked as he is, and *he's* wanting to play. He must have thought I'd come there for the fun of it. He thought I *liked* him. What a chump.

Anyway, there he was, yapping and leaping about – advancing and retreating – chasing his own little twist of a tail – getting distracted – forgetting what he was about. And me? I was fairly well fed up as you can imagine. No breakfast, no chance of a drink at the pond; this was not how I cared to spend my mornings.

At this point a couple of other dogs appeared and he was off to play with them. I was acquainted with both these dogs. One was a mild-mannered collie, but the other – some kind of mongrel terrier – had a temper. He did not take kindly to this young squirt of a puppy jumping all over him, chasing *his* tail (such as it was).

So next think I knew I had a *fight* on my hands. (At my age!) The terrier went after the puppy, I went after the terrier, the collie, out of loyalty to his pal, went after me. Then, of course, I had to take the pair of them on. And the pup was still in there, hanging on to the collie's tail at one stage, swinging around like a little Tarzan, flying through the air…bouncing. And all of us all the while growling and barking. Bedlam.

Luckily, shortly after, the owner of these other dogs arrived, separated us and put his dogs on leads. (Should have been on leads to start with.) Phew! Now I had had it. My muscles were aching, my bones were aching, my left ear had teeth marks in it and stung like the devil, and I was dying of thirst. For his part, the puppy was likewise subdued. That fight had made an impression on him, I suppose.

So home we went.

Outside the house, as we arrived, my family's car had just pulled up; the Mr and the Mrs emerging with the baby and the little girl. The big girl was on her bicycle on the pavement. The big boy was at an upstairs window, waving.

I was still leading the way, slow but sure. Only what did that pest of a puppy do? He perked up and took off, like a little bullet, yapping all the way, and hurled himself into the midst of them. And then, naturally, they all went mad as well, laughing and crying and cuddling him up. *Kissing* him even. Yuk.

What's that poem…'See the conquering hero come'? It was a bit like that, only they got the wrong hero. Not that I was jealous, of course. All *I* wanted was a bowl – make that a bucket – of water and bed.

However, as it turned out, my role in the affair was not entirely ignored. I was made a fuss of, too. Later that afternoon the Mrs presented me with a more than respectable beef bone. The big boy rubbed the top of my head in the way I liked and talked to me. How was I doing, he wanted to know, and where had I been, and what had I been up to. Not for the first time in my long life, I would dearly have loved the power of speech to tell him.

And that's about it. I was a weary old dog by this time and even that perpetual motion pup was slowing down. I retired to my basket in the kitchen. And him? He followed on shortly after and began licking my ear, the one with the teeth marks. I let him get on with it. The fact is, I was too worn out to resist. And, in its way it was, I have to confess… soothing. Medicinal even.

Hm. As to the future, well, you can't teach an old dog new tricks, you will have heard that saying. There is a lot of truth in it. There again, teaching *young* dogs *old* tricks, now that's another matter.

We'll see. Anyway, time for a snooze. I am a...sleepy old dog...hmm...altogether.

The Winner
Jean Ure

His name was Sixth of Six.

Sixth of Six, Batch B.

His fellow Batch Bs called him Sixie, or Sixer. His teacher called him 6B. There were four other batches in the class. Batch K, Batch L, Batch M, Batch P. They all had a Sixth of Six.

Batch B was a boy batch. So was Batch K. The rest were all girls. You never had a batch that was mixed. Sixer had sometimes wondered about this. He had once asked his teacher, Ms Steelman, why it was. Ms Steelman had seemed taken aback.

"That's a very strange thing to be thinking about," she had said.

It was as if she didn't expect batch kids to think.

"It's just the way things are. Don't worry about it!"

Sixer wasn't worried; he was just puzzled, that was all. There were lots of things that puzzled Sixer. What, for instance, was the difference between batch people and real people? Sixer felt like a real person! He knew he wasn't, though. Sometimes boys from outside ganged up against the batch boys and called them names.

"Clones!" "Drones!" "Reps!"

He had asked Ms Steelman what a rep was but she had told him it wasn't anything which need concern him.

"Those boys were extremely rude. They ought to know better. Don't take any notice of them!"

Ms Steelman never answered any of his questions. He was the only one who ever asked them, so you would have thought that she would have had the time. But maybe Ms Steelman didn't know herself? That was something else that Sixer sometimes wondered about.

It wasn't any use asking the rest of his batch; they just stared at him. Sixer was a bit of a strange one. Always asking questions! Always having weird thoughts.

This was another of his weird thoughts: where did batch people come from?

Where did *real* people come from?

Did they all come from the same place? He had heard that batch people came from places called *laboratories*. But he didn't know what a *laboratory* was and, as usual, nobody would tell him.

"You don't want to bother about things like that!" said Ms Steelman. It made her uncomfortable when Sixer asked his questions.

One time he asked her, "Is the others better than us is?"

She had pretended not to know what he was talking about.

"Other peoples," said Sixer. "*Real* peoples."

"Certainly not!" Ms Steelman had been quite flustered. "Nobody's better than anyone else! We all have our own abilities. Yours are just…different. That's all."

"Different *how*?" said Sixer.

But Ms Steelman wouldn't tell.

He knew one way they were different. Batch people and real people. Real people *looked* different. From each other, that is. Batch people all looked alike. Batch B boys, for instance, had sandy hair, freckled faces, little snub noses and big blue eyes. Every Batch B boy that had ever existed had been the same.

Sixer belonged to Batch B212, but only yesterday some tiddlers from a new batch B had joined the school. And they all looked alike as peas in a pod!

The teachers couldn't tell one batch boy from another. Not that it really mattered since they not only looked alike but acted alike. If you spoke to First of Six you might as well be speaking to Second, or Third, or any of the others. Except for Sixer. He was a definite oddball, was Sixer. He didn't really need to have his number sewn onto his tunic. He was the one batch boy whom everyone could recognize. The minute he opened his mouth, you knew that it was Sixer.

"6B!" said Ms Steelman. "Please concentrate! What are you doing, staring out of the window? You won't be able to stare out of the window when you're a worker!"

He had just been watching the clouds, and wondering where they came from. He turned back to his computer terminal. His batch was in Year sub-4, now. They had been through toilet training and table manners. They had learnt to dress themselves and wash themselves and brush their teeth. They had done "social graces" – please and thank you, good morning, good evening, how are you, I'm well. Now they were on to basic computer skills, which was important even for a batch kid.

Sixer enjoyed clicking his mouse and bringing different pictures on to the screen. Sometimes, being Sixer, he grew impatient and raced ahead. The rest of the class had to study things for several minutes before Ms Steelman said they could move on, but Sixer got bored looking at the same thing for too long.

"All right," said Ms Steelman. "Playtime! Off you go."

Class 4 tumbled out into the play area. Each batch tended to keep to itself. Batch B usually played football, but today Sixer wanted to do something different. Some batchmen had been moving earth with a big earth-moving machine and Sixer wanted to go and look at it. The others weren't too sure. They didn't like doing anything new or unusual.

"Come!" Sixer beckoned. "Come see!"

The batchmen had gone and so had the machine, but they had left a big deep hole behind them. Only Sixer was brave enough to jump into it. The others stood at the top, gazing down.

"Look, look!" Sixer was scrabbling at the earth, his fingers digging. "Look what I find!"

The others gaped. Sixer clambered back out of the hole. In one hand he was holding a big tin box.

"See! Look what I got!"

The others crowded round.

"What is?" said One-y.

"Buried treasure," said Sixer. No one but Sixer would have thought of a thing like that.

"Open!"

Sixer struggled with the lid. The box must have been in the earth for a very long time: the lid was stuck fast. Sixer picked up a sharp-edged stone and started bashing with it. A cheer went up as the lid came off. Now to get their hands on the treasure!

"Wait!" Very solemnly, Sixer tipped the box upside down. A scattering of objects fell to the ground.

There was:

• something square, with pages

- a little pretend person
- a strip of coloured cloth attached to a stick
- a round flat shape with a hole in the middle
- a picture.

There was also a sheet of paper, which had fluttered to the ground along with all the objects, but no one took any notice of the sheet of paper. A sheet of paper was not interesting.

This is what was written on it:

I, Susan Ann Shaw, aged 12 years and 2 months, am burying this time capsule in the back garden of my house in the year One Thousand Nine Hundred and Sixty-six. It is for people to find in the future so they will know what it was like to be a child in the 20th century. I have put in it:

A DOLL that I had when I was five

A FLAG that my brother says to include because England have just won the World Cup and he says that it is an important event

A SINGLE of the Beatles, as they are my favourite group

A PHOTOGRAPH of me and my family

A BOOK about Sir Winston Churchill because my mum says he was a great man.

Nobody picked up the sheet of paper and so it lay where it had fallen and next day the batchmen came back and churned it into the earth. But even if anyone had picked it up, they couldn't have made any sense of it. Batch kids weren't taught to read. They hadn't the brain.

"Treasure!"

One-y swooped on the little pretend person. Two-ey snatched at the strip of coloured cloth. Three-er and Four-y bagged the round flat shape with a hole in the middle. Fiver got the picture. Sixer was left with the square thing with pages.

They stood there, examining their booty. The little pretend person had strange yellow hair all fluffed up like a puffball and eyes that blinked when you tipped her up and down.

The coloured cloth was red, with a white cross. Two-ey waved it, happily. Nobody, not even Sixer, could imagine what the round flat shape with a hole in the middle could be. Four-y bowled it along the ground and all the others laughed and clapped their hands.

The picture was interesting. They examined it, carefully. It showed a man and a woman, a girl and a boy, and a big ginger-coloured animal which Sixer said was a cat. He said he had once seen a picture of one.

"They live one time in people houses."

The others didn't know whether to believe him or not. *Animals?* Living in *houses?* It didn't seem at all likely.

On the other hand, Sixer knew a great many things that they didn't.

"People! See!" Fiver pointed at them, proudly.

"Funny," said Three-er.

"Not nowadays?" Fiver looked at Sixer for confirmation. Sixer was the one they always turned to.

Sixer leant over to take a closer look.

"Not nowadays," he agreed.

"Olden days?"

"Olden days," said Sixer.

The batch soon grew tired of their treasure. Sixer was the only one who kept his safe. He didn't know what it was, exactly, but he liked the feel of it and the smell of it and the pictures inside. There were lots of little black marks, as well; lots and lots. He had a feeling that they were *words*, and that the words would tell him something if only he knew what to do with them.

He took the object to Ms Steelman. He told her how he had found it in the pit left by the batchmen.

"A book!" said Ms Steelman. "It's very old." She looked inside it. "Almost a hundred years!"

"What it for?" said Sixer.

"It's what people used to learn from before they had computers."

"I learn?" said Sixer.

"No, little Sixer!" Ms Steelman ruffled his sandy hair. "It's not for you."

"I like learn," said Sixer.

"Sixer, do you remember what I told you, the other day? How we all have different abilities? You have *other* abilities. All these words..." Ms Steelman waved a hand at a page without pictures "...they'd be far too much for you!"

Sixer's face fell.

"Don't worry about it," said Ms Steelman, kindly. "I'll keep it for you, shall I? Somewhere safe?"

"No!" Sixer rushed forward and jealously grabbed it. "Book mine! My treasure!"

All through the summer, Sixer hugged his precious treasure to him. He took it with him, everywhere he went. Very soon he knew all the pictures by heart. They all seemed to be of the same man. He started off by being young and ended up being old. Sometimes he had what looked to Sixer like a big fat sausage stuck in his mouth. The sausage seemed to be on fire, because there was smoke rising from it. He thought that maybe people in the olden days were in the habit of smoking sausages. They did do odd things. Well, for instance! Keeping animals in the house. Who ever would do that?

At the end of the summer Year sub-4 were invited to a party given by the boys and girls of Year 7 at the real school up the road. To the batch kids, it was always known as the real school. Year 4 were invited every summer. They were given tea, and little presents of the sort batch kids would enjoy. Balloons and kites and brightly-coloured balls. After tea the Year 7s always played simple games with them. Hide-and-seek or musical bumps or pass the parcel. The batch kids weren't capable of anything too complicated.

Each batch kid had its own boy or girl to look after it. A girl called Jolee-Ann was to look after Sixer. The batch kids weren't used to being separated, they preferred to stay together in their batches; but Ms Steelman said that today, at the party, they must make an effort to be on their own for just a little while. It would be good for them, she said.

"You must start learning to stand on your own two feet. After all, you won't always be together."

Sometimes, when they left school, batches were lucky enough to be given jobs as a team. Like they might all be put in the same factory, or all sent down the same sewer. That was what they hoped for. But other times they were split up, and just at first that could be frightening. Some of them were even frightened at the thought of going to the party.

Sixer wasn't frightened. Well, he was a little bit because it meant mixing with real people and he'd never had to do that before. But Sixer had an idea! He knew he wasn't supposed to have ideas. Ms Steelman was always telling him.

"Stop thinking so much, Sixer! It won't do you any good."

She meant that when he was in the factory, or down the sewer, or wherever it was they sent him, he would only make himself unhappy if he went on thinking. But Sixer couldn't help it! He was just naturally curious.

So when Jolee-Ann said to him, with her bright real-person smile, "What would you like to do?" Sixer knew exactly what he wanted.

"Read book," he said.

"Read *book*?" said Jolee-Ann.

"You not read?" said Sixer.

Jolee-Ann was indignant. "Of course I read! I've been reading since I was four years old!"

And then she blushed, because that was boasting. Just because she'd been lucky enough to be born a real person instead of a drone.

And then she blushed again. It was very rude to think of them as drones. They were *replicated people*, and just as good as anyone else.

"Please you read this for me," said Sixer, and he unzipped his top and pulled out his precious book.

Jolee-Ann took it from him, wonderingly. A drone with a book? I mean, she corrected herself, a *replicated person* with a book. It was still extraordinary!

"What it say?" said Sixer.

"It says, *Histories of Great Men: Winston Churchill*."

"What else it say?"

"You really want to know?"

Sixer nodded. What a funny little dr – *replicated person*. He seemed really eager!

"Why don't we go and sit down somewhere?" said Jolee-Ann. "Somewhere quiet. Then, if you like, I can read it to you."

So Sixer and Jolee-Ann found themselves a bench, all hidden away in a corner, and Jolee-Ann read from Sixer's book.

29

"Winston Churchill was born in 1874. He was greatly beloved of the British people and became a great statesman and a great war leader, known affectionately as Winnie. At school he was not regarded as particularly bright, but in spite of that –"

Sixer listened, intently. Sometimes there were words he hadn't heard before and didn't understand, but all the same, it was exciting! Jolee-Ann was telling this whole story from the marks on the page!

"I like do that," said Sixer, when she'd finished.

"What, read?" said Jolee-Ann. She almost laughed. The idea of a dr – a *replicated person* being able to read! But she stopped herself, just in time. "Shall I try and teach you?" she said.

"Yes, please!" said Sixer.

All the other kids were running about with their balloons, or flying their kites, but Sixer went on sitting there with Jolee-Ann the whole afternoon. By the time Ms Steelman came looking for him, to take him back to school, he could write the first ten letters of the alphabet and spell the words *big*, *fig* and *jig*. He could hardly wait to tell Ms Steelman!

"I write words," he said. "Look!"

Ms Steelman looked. "Good gracious me!" she said. "Who taught you that?"

"Jolee-Ann. She read my book."

And he told Ms Steelman what the book was about. A great man called Winston Churchill who was no good at school but went on to be prime minister and win a big war and everybody loved him and called him Winnie.

"Why did they do that, I wonder?" said Ms Steelman. "Was it because his name was Winston, do you think?"

But Sixer said no. They had called him Winnie because he had *won*. Because he was a *winner*.

"This what I going be," said Sixer. "I going be like Winston Churchill." He clutched his book: his precious book. "I going to be a *WINNER*!"

The Ghost House
Berlie Doherty

They were running after her, cackling and laughing, hissing, screaming curses. She had nowhere to hide from them. If she ran to the dormitory they would follow her there and scatter her clothes over the beds and out of the window. They would climb trees after her, crawl under bushes. They always found her. There was no escape. "Pipit," they called, "Fly, little bird. Pipit, Pipit, Pipit."

"Leave me alone!" she begged, turning quickly to face them.

"Fly, Pipit, fly!" shouted Astrid, the leader of the pack, and they closed in on her again, mouths wide open, arms outstretched, chirruping like the bird that she was named after. Pipit covered her ears with her hands and ran again, through the trees with their long spiky fronds, over the long spines of fallen palm branches. Above her head, birds with ragged wings chattered and shrieked as if they were joining in the chase.

And suddenly, there in front of her was the Ghost House. It was just a long bamboo shack without windows. Why would a ghost need windows? But the ghosts lived there, sure enough. Everybody knew that. Nobody ever went to the Ghost House, not even the bravest of the orphans, not even Astrid. But there was nowhere else to hide, and the pack was screeching behind her. The door swung open. Pipit had no choice. She ran straight up the wooden steps and through the door into the darkness of the shack. And the baying voices behind her fell silent, as if they were choked with holy wonder.

The ghosts loomed out of the darkness. One of them came gliding towards Pipit, dressed in a long white sarong that swished slightly like the breath of wind across the rice fields. The ghost's face was as pale as a lotus flower. And, as the ghost bent down towards her, Pipit saw that it had no eyes.

31

Pipit screamed. She covered up her face and screamed. She felt the ghost's hands touching hers, and still she screamed. She felt the ghost's cool fingers stroking her cheeks. "You poor child," said the ghost. "Don't cry. Please don't be frightened."

Pipit stopped screaming and drew in her breath sharply. It was the first time anyone had spoken kindly to her since she arrived at the orphanage. She felt the ghost stroking her hair, and the gentle touch was so soothing that her sobs shuddered away to nothing. "There now," the ghost murmured. "That's better, isn't it? We don't like to hear anyone crying, do we?"

There was a rumble of voices round the room. Now Pipit could see quite clearly the other ghosts in the room, sitting on the long beds that were lined round the walls. The ghosts stood up and came towards her, stretching out their hands to touch her. She backed away, terror rising up in her again like a wild cat, but as she turned to the door she remembered Astrid and the other taunting children, waiting outside to chase her and catch her. She hesitated.

"What are you afraid of?" the first ghost asked. Her voice was soothing and kind. Pipit shuddered. Her breath came in little wounded shreds. "The orphans," she whispered. "They never leave me alone. They hate me."

"That's a shame," the ghost said. "Hate is a wicked thing."

The other ghosts murmured in agreement.

"But why do they hate you?" the first ghost asked again. "Did you do something wicked to make them hate you?"

"Because I had a letter." Pipit knew very well why the children in the orphanage hated her. She was not an orphan. Her body shuddered with sobs as she remembered the day the men from the village had come running from the coconut palms, where they had been cutting branches for the boss's roof. They were carrying a bundle of rags heaped on a stretcher of palm branches roped together. They put down the stretcher at their door, shouting for Pipit's mother. "Ibu Tiki, Ibu Tiki, Pak is dead." And her mother had run out of the house, screaming, clutching her new baby in her arms,

and Pipit and her brothers and sisters had stood in ghastly silence round the bundle of rags that was their father. But he wasn't dead. He was a ghost without a voice and without the strength to lift his hand to his face, but he was alive. The boss's wife came every day to peer at him and shake her head, and at last she told Pipit's mother that she had thought of a plan to help her.

"You must send Pipit to the orphanage," she said. "I will arrange it for you. She will learn to read and write there, and when she leaves she will be able to work and earn money to help you." And Pipit's mother had agreed with her. She held Pipit close and told her that it would only be for a few years, that she was lucky to have the opportunity, and that the boss's wife was doing them a great kindness.

It didn't feel like a kindness to Pipit. It felt like a punishment.

She was sent on the bus on a long journey, and came to the big orphanage house that was full of taunting children and scolding nuns, and she cried every night to go home again. Three months later, Pipit received a parcel of sweets from her mother, and a letter telling her that the baby was standing on her own now, that her father was managing to feed himself, that the mango trees by the river were heavy with fruit, that everybody missed her. She carried the letter round with her all the time, and at every opportunity took it from the knot in her sarong and uncreased it and read it out loud. But she knew in her heart that her mother hadn't written the letter. She would have dictated it shyly to the boss's wife, laughing with pleasure as her words took shape on the page. There was only one word that her mother could have written herself, and that was the very first of the letter. *Pipit.* The scrawled letters ambled across the line like ants on the march.

"And that's why they hate me," Pipit told the ghost. "Because of my letter. And they keep chasing me. They won't leave me alone."

The ghost nodded and sighed. "But you can obviously run faster than them," she chuckled. "We heard you."

Pipit stole another glance at the strange pale face with its empty eye sockets. The face was smiling. It gave her the courage to carry on. "They do other things," she whispered. "They steal my clothes. They wipe mud on them. My mother sent me a present of sweets and peanuts and they stole them and ate them. But the worst thing was … was when they tore up my mother's letter. She didn't write it herself," she added. "Only one word. Pipit. That's what she called me, after the little bird."

"And don't they ever get letters?"

"Of course not," said Pipit. "There's no one to write them."

There was a deep silence in the Ghost House, a deep, sad, empty silence. One of the ghosts started humming, very softly, making a rippling sound in the back of her throat. Another joined in, and then another. The eyeless ghost who had been talking to Pipit began to sing in a full strong voice. Deep in the shadows another struck the tinkling keys of a xylophone. The eyeless ghost clapped her hands softly and began to dance.

"Dance with me Pipit, dance with me," she said, stretching out her hands, and, bewildered, half laughing, half afraid, Pipit allowed the cool, soft hands of the ghost to hold her own and to swing her round.

And she danced for the home she had left behind, for the bamboo huts behind the palm trees, for the river where she swam with her brothers and sisters and where she washed herself every morning and every night, where her mother scrubbed their clothes and stretched them across rocks to dry in the bright sun. She danced for her father lying silently on his rough bed, and for the boss's kind wife who had written her a letter with her own blue biro. She danced for the haunting sound of the call to prayer from the distant mosque. She danced for the sound of crickets and frogs singing at night on the river bank, and the rain cascading like fountains between the fronds of the palm trees, and the mist like a dog's breath rising from the mountains. She danced to the sound of the morning bird singing *Pipit, Pipit*; and she laughed out loud.

Outside the Ghost House the orphan children looked at each other in amazement. They had expected to see Pipit run screaming for help long before now. When she didn't, they whispered to one another that she must have been eaten by the ghosts. They crept away until they could watch the house from a safe distance, crouching under a spreading shrub. Now there was singing coming from the Ghost House, and the soft patter of bare feet dancing, and surely the sound of a child laughing. Could that be Pipit?

It was Astrid who stood up first. "I'm going back," she said. "I'm bored of chasing Pipit. It's a silly game." And they ran down the dusty track to the orphanage, shrieking to hide their fears, chasing the scraggy cats up the trees, kicking the matted husks of coconuts that lay on the ground.

"Are you really ghosts?" Pipit asked, when the dancing had stopped.

The women laughed. "Ghosts?" the first one chuckled. "No, I'm not a ghost. I'm Beti. I'm an orphan. We're all orphans, same as everyone else here."

"Except me," Pipit reminded her.

"What makes you think we're ghosts?"

"Because this is the Ghost House," said Pipit, uncertainly "Everyone calls it the Ghost House. And because – " she hesitated.

"Go on," said Beti, gently.

"Because you haven't got any eyeballs."

Beti laughed, a lovely infectious laugh that made Pipit laugh, too, in spite of herself.

"I was born without eyes," Beti said. "It's as simple as that. I'm blind. We're all blind in this house. Even though we're grown up the nuns let us stay here because we can't work and we can't find our way around the world."

Pipit felt ashamed. She remembered how frightened she had felt when she ran into the Ghost House, how she had backed away screaming when Beti had come to her and stroked her hair, how terrified she had been of the face without eyes.

"Perhaps you should go to your lessons now," Beti said. "We don't want you getting into trouble with the nuns, do we?"

"But can I come again?"

"Of course you can. I'll tell you some stories. Would you like that?"

"Yes, please," said Pipit. "My mother used to tell me stories."

"But listen, Pipit. I don't want you to come here just because you're running away from the other children. Do you understand what I mean?"

"I think so," said Pipit, but she didn't, and Beti could tell she didn't.

"Running away won't help you. I'm blind, but I can't run away from my blindness. It's with me every day of my life. And the children out there who have no parents, they can't run away from being orphans."

"I know," said Pipit. "But when I'm frightened, I just can't help it."

Beti nodded. "Of course you were frightened. You were screaming loud enough to wake the jungle up! But you can't run away from fear. You have to face it. You're not still frightened, are you?"

"Not of you," Pipit said. "But I'm still afraid of Astrid and the others."

"Astrid most of all?"

Pipit thought of Astrid with her wild hair, her loud mocking voice.

"Yes, Astrid's the one I'm frightened of."

"I don't think you should be afraid of Astrid. She's lost more than you will ever lose. Just remember that, next time she tries to frighten you. Now I'm going to ask you to be very brave. I want you to come back tomorrow and listen to a very scary story. Will you dare to come?"

Pipit laughed. "Yes, please!"

"Off you go then, little Pipit."

Pipit ran from the Ghost House as if she was a bird that had suddenly learnt to fly. Darkness had fallen. Behind her she could hear the music of Beti's house; the quiet chiming gongs and xylophones of the gamelan music, the sweet high sound of Beti's voice singing. She hugged her happiness to herself. The gaunt walls of the Convent House reared up beyond the trees, lights flooding from its windows. She could see the windows of the huge dormitory that she shared with Astrid and the other girls. Somebody was standing at the window watching her, a child's shape dark against the lit room, a girl with wild hair. She knew it was Astrid. It was then that Pipit thought of the bravest thing she could do. She took a slow, deep breath and went up the steps into the orphanage.

That night, at study time, the children watched her silently as she entered the library. There was no giggling, no grinning shared glances, no whispered name calling, no chirrups mocking her name. With a kind of silent awe they watched her as she looked slowly round the room. She opened her homework books and began to write, as the other children were doing. When I go home, she thought, I will teach my brothers and sisters to write. And my mother. She stared in front of her. In her head she could hear the sweet, steady chanting of Beti's voice singing, calm and warm and happy. How could she live here and be happy? How could she be blind and be happy? How could she bear to be an orphan?

She took a piece of paper from her schoolbook and began to write a letter. She wrote slowly and carefully, in her best writing. She folded up the finished letter and wrote the address on the front. Then she walked over to where Astrid was sitting and put it on her desk. Her heart was pounding in case the study nun saw her, or in case Astrid tore up the letter or laughed out loud at her, her loud cruel taunting laugh. But Astrid didn't laugh. She cradled the letter in her hands for a moment, and then, very slowly, very carefully, as if she was savouring every moment of it, she opened it up. Her eyes widened in amazement as she stared at the words that Pipit had written on the piece of paper.

Dear Astrid,
Will you come to the Ghost House with me tomorrow?
Pipit.

Astrid folded up her letter and slipped it inside her school book. She didn't say anything, didn't look at Pipit, just carried on with her work as if nothing had happened. But that night, when Pipit went to the dormitory she found a note on her mattress with a single word written on it.

Yes.

They set off after lessons the next afternoon. Neither of them spoke, and they walked slightly apart, heads down. As they left the convent gardens and went through the shady palm grove Pipit's heart began to beat faster, remembering her terror of the day before. She stole a quick glance at Astrid, but the girl's face was set and determined. The door of the shack was open. Pipit went in quickly, and after a moment's hesitation, Astrid followed her.

Beti came forward to meet them. Pipit heard Astrid's quick, surprised gasp. But she didn't scream, as Pipit had done. She glanced quickly at Pipit and then back at Beti, searching her strange, eyeless face.

40

"Are there two of you?" Beti asked. She reached out and touched each of the girls lightly on the head.

"I've brought Astrid," said Pipit.

Beti grasped Astrid's hands in both her own. "Welcome," she said. "Welcome, both of you."

Astrid gazed round her, still saying nothing. She was no longer the noisy, boastful leader of the pack. She was unsure of herself, glancing every now and again at Pipit to see what she should do. But one thing was certain. She wasn't running away.

"We've been making cakes, haven't we, Beti? In case Pipit came today," said a tiny white-haired woman. "Coconut cakes," she added, smacking her lips.

"Good job we made plenty," Beti laughed. "Astrid's a big girl. I bet she could eat a plateful on her own."

Astrid found her voice at last. "I love coconut cakes. They're my favourite."

"And mine," put in Pipit, quickly. They looked at each other shyly.

Because some of the women could remember a time before they were blind, when darkness used to frighten them, they lit a lantern and placed it in the middle of plates of cakes on the table. The girls sat next to each other and ate in silence, watching the women, staring round from time to time as the room took shape in the flickering light. It was bare except for the beds and the cooking area, but over one of the beds was a shelf of heavy books.

"Are they real books?" Astrid asked, and Beti stood up and lifted one down from the shelf.

"This is a Braille book of stories," she said. "This is how blind people read."

41

"Beti isn't really a ghost," said Pipit. "She's blind."

Astrid giggled. "I didn't think ghosts could make coconut cakes! Can you tell us a story, Beti?"

Astrid and Pipit watched in fascinated silence as Beti ran her finger quickly over the dotted cells and began to tell a story.

"There was once a boy called Ismael. One day he went to the market to buy fruit for his mother. He saw an old man stooping over a cart that was full of fists of bananas, those tiny ones that are so sweet you would think the bees had made them. Ismael loved these best of all, and he asked the man if he could buy a bunch. The old man picked a bunch and turned to give them to Ismael – " Beti stopped. "Oh, but that's a bit scary. I don't think I want to frighten you. I'll tell you a different story, shall I?"

She turned the heavy pages over. "This one's my favourite. The story of Lori Jongrengg."

"A long time ago," she said, "when magicians lived in the dark places of the world, there was a beautiful princess called Lori Jongrengg, the Fair One. A prince came to ask her to marry him and she said, yes, she would marry him if he agreed to build her a thousand temples in one night. She didn't like him, you see, and she knew that such a thing was impossible. So she went to bed and slept well. But during the night her maid woke her up and said, 'Princess, princess, the magicians of the night are helping him. He's built nine hundred and ninety nine temples already, and he's about to start his thousandth.' The princess jumped out of her bed and called all her maids together, and asked them to gather all their friends and sisters and help her to pound rice. The noise of their pounding drummed round all the walls of the city and woke up the cockerels in their yards. The cockerels crowed in unison, and when the magicians heard the cockerels crowing they thought dawn must be coming, and they were so afraid of the daylight that they fled to all their dark places and hid there. And the prince knew that the princess had won, because the thousandth temple hadn't been built."

42

"So what happened to her?" asked Pipit, even though she knew the story very well.

"The prince agreed that he couldn't ask her to marry him, but because she had cheated him he turned her to stone. She became the thousandth temple. And there she stands to this very day, the beautiful temple of Lori Jongrengg in Prambanan."

Pipit clapped her hands. "I know that story. I love it. My mother – " she stopped and looked at Astrid. "My mother used to tell me that story."

"So did mine," said Astrid. "Before she died, she used to tell it to me."

Beti closed up the Braille book. "There's so many stories in here," she said. "Will you come back again to hear some more?"

"Yes, please," whispered Astrid.

"I can hear the night noises outside. You ought to be getting back to the convent house."

"Just one more story! Please!" Astrid begged.

"The story of Ismael!" said Pipit. "We won't be scared, will we, Astrid?"

Beti leant forward and blew out the lantern light. "Seeing as you're so brave, and you don't believe in ghosts any more." She lowered her voice, making it shivery with promise.

The women around her folded their hands and dropped into silence. Outside, crickets chirred in the darkness.

"The old man in the market handed Ismael the bunch of sweet bananas, and he dropped them in fright. For when the man looked up, he had no face! It's true! Ismael screamed like a monkey and ran away from the market, ran along the jungle path, ran and ran, screaming and shouting, till he could run no more. He collapsed on the ground. Some villagers clustered round him and asked him what was the matter, why was he screaming, and Ismael told them. 'It was terrible,' he said. 'I saw a man with no face!' He felt a hand on his shoulder. 'Did he look like me?' a voice asked. Ismael turned round, and his heart turned to stone inside him, because when the speaker lifted his hood – he had no face."

Astrid and Pipit jumped up, clutching each other.

"Goodnight, little friends," Beti laughed.

But Pipit and Astrid had already gone; stumbling out of the Ghost House, down the steps, through the palm grove, down the dusty paths and across the lawns that led to the warm lights of the Convent House. Screaming and shrieking with laughter they danced, hand in hand.

With thanks to Mathilde Tumengungg in Indonesia.

How I Stole Your Brain
Stephen Law

Cast your mind back about three months. Do you remember having a rather disturbed night's sleep? That was the night that I, Setrac, stole your brain.

I see you don't believe me. But it's true. You're currently in my laboratory here on Proteus, one of the moons of Neptune.

In fact, you're sat right here beside me, on my desk, next to a plate of sandwiches. You can't see or hear or touch me, of course. That's why I have to communicate with you through this book.

Here, let me draw a scene for you.

There, that's how things *really* are. You can see me seated at the desk. To the right is Robbie, my robot helper, carrying a cup of tea. Now look more closely at my desk. Next to the sandwiches. The brain with the leads attached?

Yes, that's you.

I realise, of course, that it *seems* to you as if you are still on Earth. You even think that you are holding a book in your hands, don't you? But you're wrong. This book is not real. The time has come for me to reveal the truth.

But before I explain what has happened to you, I had better explain what brains *do*.

What brains do

Let's use my Neptunian televiewer to observe an Earthling. I'll point it at Fred. That's him down there.

As you can observe, Fred is looking at some cakes. What's going on inside Fred as he experiences those cakes? I'll zoom in on Fred's head so we can see what's happening.

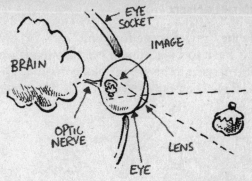

Light is bouncing off the cakes and entering Fred's eye to form an image. This image is causing electrical signals to move down a nerve (called the *optic nerve*) into Fred's brain. And that, in turn, is causing Fred to see the cakes.

Aha! It looks like Fred has decided he wants to eat one of the cakes. What's happening now? Electric signals are coming out of Fred's brain and travelling down his arm. That's making the muscles move, which in turn is making Fred's hand grab the cake, like this…

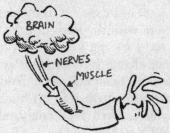

So you can see that Fred's brain is really a sort of *central control room*: signals *come in* from Fred's senses allowing him to experience the world around him; other signals *go out* to move his body about.

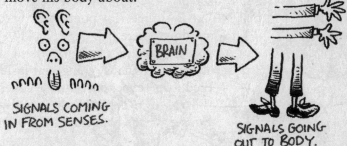

SIGNALS COMING IN FROM SENSES.

SIGNALS GOING OUT TO BODY.

Artificial eyes

But does it have to be a human eye that sends signals down Fred's optic nerve into his brain? No, it doesn't. Fred's normal eyes could have been replaced with little TV cameras instead.

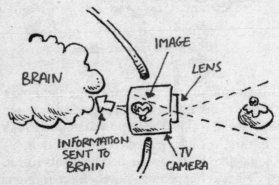

These cameras could send the same signals to Fred's brain that normal eyes send. So the world seen through artificial eyes would look just the same to Fred.

Having an eye on the end of a stick

In fact, in some ways having little TV camera eyes could be a big advantage. Suppose we were to give Fred TV camera eyes. And suppose these eyes were attached to his brain with extra-long cables. Then Fred could take out an eye and hold it in his hand.

Or he could have an eye on the end of a stick – perfect for finding the coin he dropped under the sofa.

Having a robot body

Actually, there's no reason why we couldn't replace *all* Fred's sense organs with artificial ones. We could even replace his *entire body*. Here's how.

Suppose Fred's brain is removed and fitted into a new robot body.

Then his old human body is destroyed. But that doesn't matter. For Fred's new robot body keeps his brain alive. It also sends into his brain the same sort of signals sent by his old human body. So Fred's robot body gives him experiences just like the ones his old body gave him. He can enjoy cream cakes, listen to music, and smell flowers.

Everything seems just the same.

And because Fred's new robot body responds to the signals coming out of his brain in the same way his old body used to, Fred can walk and talk just as before.

MMMM DELICIOUS CAKE!

In fact, this robot body could even have fantastic new powers. Fred could be given X-ray vision and superhuman strength.

He could be made to run faster than a bullet, or fly like a rocket. There's almost no limit to what someone with a robot body might do!

How to relax in virtual reality

Now that I've explained about brains, we can say 'Goodbye' to Fred and turn off the televiewer.

But there's one more thing I need to tell you about before I explain what has happened to *your* brain. I need to tell you about *virtual reality*.

A virtual reality is a world generated by a computer. Perhaps you've played a computer game in which you drive a car round a racetrack or fly a plane through the sky. As you know, the cars, racetrack and planes don't actually exist. They are all virtual.

Now the kind of virtual worlds we Neptunians have created are much more advanced than anything developed by you Earthlings. Indeed, we have learned how to *immerse our brains directly in virtual reality*. Here's how we do it.

Like most Neptunians, I have a little socket fitted to the back of my neck. The socket is connected up to where the nerves running in and out of my brain join the rest of my body. And I can use this socket to connect my brain up to a powerful super-computer. All I have to do is plug a cable from the computer into my socket and flip a switch at the back of my neck.

Now this computer runs a virtual reality programme. Here's how it works. I lie down on a bed next to the computer and plug myself in. Then I reach round to the back of my neck and flip that switch. Of course, the moment I flip the switch my body goes limp: I've just disconnected my body from my brain.

But that's not how it seems to me. It seems to me that I can still move my body. Suppose I try to waggle my fingers in front of my face. The computer registers the finger-waggling signals coming out of my brain. It then sends back to my brain just the sort of signals it would receive from my eyes if

I were really waggling my fingers in front of my face. So it looks to me just like I'm waggling my fingers in front of my face. But of course, the fingers I see waggling are *virtual* fingers, not real fingers. My *real* hand lies motionless on the bed.

In fact, my computer is so powerful that it can generate a *whole virtual environment* for me. I can see virtual trees, smell virtual flowers, even eat virtual food.

Switching over to a virtual world can be a pleasant way to spend time. I can even choose what my virtual body looks like! In fact, I spent my last summer vacation exploring a planet made entirely out of marshmallow, while looking like Elvis Presley.

Why I, Setrac, stole your brain
Now I shall tell you what happened to your brain. Prepare yourself.

Every year there's a *Grand Neptunian Virtual Reality Challenge* held here on Proteus. This year, the challenge was to build a virtual Earth. The first computer to fool a human brain into thinking it was still on Earth for three months would win a lifetime's supply of roast shiblits – a Neptunian delicacy. Believe me, they are delicious!

I entered the competition with my computer programme *Earth Simulator II*. That's right, *Earth Simulator II* is designed to simulate your home planet down to the very last detail!

Once I finished *Earth Simulator II*, I needed a human brain to test it. That's where you come in. Here's what I did.

First of all, I flew from Neptune to Earth in my flying saucer.

I parked outside where you live (being careful not to hit that tree), and crept into your bedroom. There I drugged you and performed a delicate surgical operation. I opened your skull, severed your brain stem and optic nerves, and removed your brain. Then I placed your sleeping brain in a jar of life supporting liquid.

After that, I flew back to Neptune. Currently, your brain is sitting on top of a bench in my science laboratory many millions of miles from Earth.

So why does it seem to you that you are still on Earth? Because you are plugged into *Earth Simulator II*, of course!

Currently, all the electrical impulses coming out of your brain are being sent to *Earth Simulator II*. *Earth Simulator II* monitors these impulses and then sends back exactly

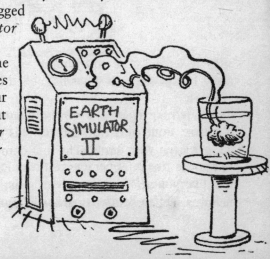

the same patterns of impulses that your brain would receive if you were still in your body back on Earth. So it seems to you just as if you are still on Earth.

Go on: test out *Earth Simulator II*! Put one of your hands up in front of your face and waggle your fingers.

It looks just as if you are waggling your fingers in front of your face, doesn't it? But the fingers you now see waggling are actually *virtual* fingers, not real fingers. They're part of the programme. In fact, you don't have real fingers any more. In fact, you don't have a body. You are a disembodied brain sitting in a glass jar.

Everything you see around you is an illusion. But the illusion is so good, you *can't tell* it's an illusion. Fantastic eh? Not even this book is real. Yes, I know you *think* you can feel the texture of the paper under your thumb and sense the weight of the book in your hands. But it's a *virtual* book. I've put it inside this virtual reality so I can explain what has happened.

Thanks to you, I've finally won *The Grand Neptunian Virtual Reality Trophy!* Here, let me draw it for you.

Isn't it great? I'm very proud!

How I, Setrac, replaced your brain with a machine
Of course, none of the people you've met recently have been real, not even your friends.

I am the first *real* person you have come across for some time. Everyone else has been virtual (a bit like Lara Croft or the Super Mario Brothers, only much more convincing).

REAL FRIENDS   VIRTUAL FRIENDS

Maybe you are wondering how your *real* friends and family reacted on discovering your brainless body in your bed?

Well, don't worry. I didn't just leave your body lying there with an empty head. I fitted it with a replacement brain. Using advanced Neptunian technology, I created a clever electronic gadget that responds to patterns of electrical stimulation in exactly the same way that your real brain does. So the next morning, your body got out of bed just as usual. Right now, your body is alive and well and doing all the things it used to do. The artificial brain is controlling all of its movements. So none of your friends or family are any the wiser. No one knows you've gone!

Your last days on Proteus
But don't panic: I've just *borrowed* your brain. I don't plan to keep it. In fact, this is your last day here on Proteus. Tonight, after you fall asleep, I will fly you back to Earth, take that electronic brain out of your head and put your real brain back. I will reconnect all your nerves and other plumbing so that, when you wake up, everything will be back to normal. You will wake up among your *real* friends and relatives back on the *real* Earth.

As you finish these last few sentences and begin the rest of your final day here on Proteus, do please feel free to test the *Earth Simulator II* to the full. If you discover a flaw in the programme, even a little one (for example, you might notice that your best friends eyes aren't *quite* the right colour, or that your bedroom is a *tiny* bit bigger than it should be, or that your parents are now speaking with the vaguest *hint* of a Japanese accent) would you be kind enough to let me know? You can just shout, 'Setrac, I have found a flaw!' and then describe it. Alternatively, you can fill in this form:

I will continue to monitor your brain and will detect your message.

Thanks again for testing *Earth Simulator II* and helping me to win that trophy. I'm off to enjoy a big plate of shiblits. Goodbye!

Is this story true? It is extremely difficult for you to tell. Actually, there is one way in which you might be able to tell – can you guess what it is? (Answer at bottom of page.)

For other philosophical puzzles like this one, try The Philosophy Files *(Dolphin paperback, for both children and adults) or* The Philosophy Gym *(Hodder-Headline, for adults), both by Stephen Law.*

If this story is true, then tomorrow, when you wake up in the real world, this book will no longer be around. For if the story is true, Setrac created this book as a part of the virtual Earth: it doesn't exist in the real world. But hang on a minute. What if Setrac was lying about putting your brain back? Perhaps he plans to leave you connected to *Earth Simulator II* forever! Is there any way in which you will be able to tell that you aren't still on Proteus? I don't think there is!

The Boy Who Swims Forever
David Almond

Deepest night. The lighthouse light was turning. It sent its beam across the sea and then the land and then the sea again.

Lucy watched from her window. She lived there, right along the beach beside the lighthouse.

When the light came, she saw the rocks, the rock pools, the islands and the water.

Then the darkness came again.

She saw the light and then the dark, the light and then the dark.

Miles out, there were great ships heading north.

Above everything were millions and millions of stars.

Lucy held her hands across her eyes. She felt her tears on her fingers. This only made her cry again. Her dad had gone fishing in the north and she missed him, she missed him, she missed him.

Once, he used to go out in a small ship. He didn't go far. He went out in the morning and came back with his fish at night. During the day she could look out and see his small ship out among the islands. She could see him casting his nets and pulling them in again. She could see him coming back to the harbour with his fish. But there were no fish now. Her dad said the sea had died and the fish had gone.

Lucy had told him it couldn't be true.

"How could the whole sea die?" she said.

He hugged her tight.

"We didn't care for it enough," he said. "We took the good things out and we put bad things in and we let it die."

Lucy thought of him far away in the north. The boat he went in seemed huge to Lucy, but she knew that in the north it was just a tiny thing. Everything was bigger there. There were icebergs as big as villages, waves higher than houses, fish called halibut as big as men. Up there sometimes the sky was on fire with the Northern Lights. Sometimes it was filled with the booming and banging and flashing of great storms. Up there the fishermen worked for days and nights on end. They were worn out. They were as scared as their children. They dreamed only of getting safely home again.

Lucy watched the lighthouse beam sweeping across the sea again.

The beam seemed endless.

Once she asked him, "Does it reach all the way to the north?"

"No," he said. "But when I come south again, I look out for it, and when I see it I know I'll be safe and with you soon."

Lucy rubbed her eyes. She saw a shooting star fall towards the sea. She rested her head on the windowsill. There were seashells and sea urchins and bits of dried-out seaweed there. There was the white pebble shaped just like a girl that her dad had brought up in his net one day. She held the pebble and remembered how he had put it in her hand and said it was a gift from the sea to her. He said the pebble's name was Lucy Two, Lucy from the sea. She smelt sea and salt and she felt sand against her cheek. She closed her eyes. She knew she should go back to bed. She knew she should go to sleep. Her mother had said she'd wear herself out with worrying, and it wouldn't bring him home any sooner. But how *could* she sleep, when she was so scared, and when the lighthouse beam kept coming back and coming back?

She started to dream. She saw huge waves, huge storms, huge icebergs. She heard her dad shouting that the fish were so big that the ship would sink. She saw the lighthouse beam spinning faster and faster and faster…

And she woke up again, and rubbed her eyes, and looked out again.

There was somebody on the rocks.

Lucy stared. She was certain there was somebody on the rocks. She waited for the light to come round again, to shine on the rocks and show her who was there.

The light came, and it shone, and she saw nothing.

She looked again, into the darkness, and she saw it again. Somebody on the rocks, beside the rock pools. A child, moving from pool to pool, sometimes stopping, reaching down into the pools of water.

It was a boy, a pale and skinny boy.

The light came again, and it shone on the rocks again, and she saw nothing.

He could only be seen in the dark. He crouched on the rocks. He reached down into a pool of water. The light of the stars shone on his back. Lucy pressed her face against the window and she saw the boy look up to her. She held her breath.

Then the light came again, and he couldn't be seen again.

Lucy put her dressing gown on. She tiptoed out of her room and out of the house. She tiptoed into the night and onto the rocks. She felt the breeze and the cold spray on her face and the sharp rocks on her feet. She held Lucy Two in her hand. She stared into the night.

"Who's there?" she whispered. "Who's there?"

She saw nothing. She heard nothing but the slap and splash of the sea. The lighthouse beam came and went again. She shivered. She told herself she must have been dreaming.

Then she saw him. He was right beside her. He was kneeling by a pool and reaching down into the water. He looked up at her and she saw that he had been crying as well.

"Who are you?" she whispered.

He said nothing. He lifted something out of the water and held it up to the starlight.

"Look," he said.

She knelt beside him. He had a starfish in his hand. It had four long legs and one that was short and stunted.

"What happened?" she asked him.

He shook his head and said nothing.

She saw that he had hardly any hair. There were sores and patches of black oil on his skin.

He gently touched the starfish.

"I swim for miles," he said. "And I see no fish but wounded ones."

She touched the starfish, too.

"What's gone wrong?" she asked him.

"It lost a leg. But it will grow again. It will look as if nothing was ever wrong."

He stretched down, and put the starfish into the water.

"You'll have to look after it," he said.

"Where have you come from?" she asked, but the lighthouse beam came round again, and for a moment the boy was gone.

For a moment there was just Lucy kneeling on the rocks with Lucy Two in her hand.

She saw another shooting star, falling to the sea.

In the darkness, Lucy watched the boy picking at the sores and the black oil on his skin. She saw how his skin was stretched between his fingers, like the skin on the feet of seabirds. She saw how the skin on his back was scaly like the skin of fish.

"How far do you swim?" she asked him.

"Forever and forever and forever."

"As far as the icebergs? Where the ships are tiny and the waves are huge? Where the fish are as big as men and the men are as scared as children?"

"Yes," he said. "As far as that."

61

He looked down into the pool again.

"Look after the starfish," he said. "Come out every day and see that the leg is growing and that nothing's going wrong."

"What can I do for it?" she said.

"Nothing. Just care for it. Watch over it."

"What can I give it?"

"Give it nothing. Take nothing away from it. Just watch over it. Just let it grow."

And the light came again, and he was gone again.

Lucy looked towards her dark house. She looked towards the north. She thought of waves as big as houses and she shivered and cried.

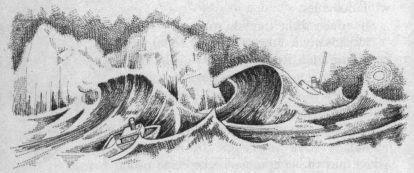

"My dad's in the north," she said. "My dad's in a tiny ship where the icebergs and the storms and the Northern Lights are."

The boy stared at her. His eyes were dark and watery and they were filled with stars.

"Tears are salt water," he said. "They show that the sea is inside you."

"My dad's as scared as I am," she said.

The boy touched her cheek. His fingers were icy cold.

"He wants to see the lighthouse again and come back to me again," she said.

She watched the boy licking his fingers.

"He'll be gone for days and days and days," she said.

"Tears are the sea trickling from your eyes," he said.

He licked his fingers.

"I have awful dreams," she said. "I see the icebergs and the waves and the fish as big as men. I see my dad going down into the waves and never coming back again."

The boy touched her cheek again.

The lighthouse beam came back. Still she felt his gentle fingers on her cheek.

"Who are you?" she whispered when the light had gone.

"I'm the boy who swims forever and forever in the sea."

"My dad says the sea is dead."

"The sea is wounded like the starfish."

"He says we take the good things out and put bad things in and all the living things are dying."

The boy showed Lucy the sores and the oil stains on his scaly skin.

"The sea is wounded just like me," he said.

He touched her eyes and licked his fingers.

"The sea is wounded just like you," he said.

She held her breath and watched him. "Could you take me swimming?" she said. "Could you take me to where my dad is? To the icebergs and the waves and the fish as big as men?"

He shook his head.

"You'd die," he said. "The sea is like ice and the icebergs are jagged and the fish could swallow you whole."

The light passed, the dark came back, and still he was shaking his head and saying no.

Lucy held out her hand and showed him the white pebble shaped just like a girl.

"This is Lucy Two," she said.

He reached into her hand and touched the pebble and told her it was beautiful

"My dad brought her up in his net one day," she said.

"He said she's Lucy from the sea."

She looked out across the islands and the water. She saw that the darkness at the edge of the world was fading. Soon the stars, that can only be seen at night, would start to go out.

She stared down into the pool, looking for the starfish, but the water was too dark, and it couldn't be seen.

"I'll come out each day," she said. "I'll watch over the starfish. I'll see that nothing goes wrong."

Now the boy looked across the sea. He saw the light growing at the world's edge. Lucy reached out and touched his cold scaly skin. She touched his fingers like those of seabirds. She touched the sores and the black oil. She told him that he was beautiful.

"Where do you go in the day?" she asked.

"I swim forever and forever."

"Will you take Lucy Two to where the icebergs are? Will you take her to my dad so that Lucy from the sea is with him and so he won't feel so scared."

The boy reached into her hand and took the pebble from her.

He disappeared when the beam came round again.

In the darkness afterwards there was more light shining from the edge of the world and the boy was fading.

He stood up beside the pool. He was smiling. The final stars were shining in his dark eyes.

"Will you swim back here again?" she asked.

"One night," he said. "In the deepest night."

He walked across the rocks past the pools towards the sea. She stared after him. He slipped into the water. He faded to nothing. The beam came round again and slowly the sky was filled with light.

Lucy shivered. She felt the cold spray on her face. She tiptoed back across the sharp rocks. She tiptoed back into the house and into her room. She lay sleeping in her bed, dreaming of the boy and Lucy Two swimming to the north.

The lighthouse beam stopped turning. The stars went out. Daylight shone on the seashells and sea urchins and seaweed on her windowsill.

Soon her mother was calling her.

"Lucy! Lucy! Lucy!"

Every day, Lucy went out to the pool. She stared down and saw the starfish there. She saw the four long legs and the one that was short and stunted. Every day the short leg grew a little longer. Soon it would be as if nothing had ever been wrong.

She told her mother that the sea was not really dead. She said it was wounded, and it needed to be watched and cared for. She said that one day her dad would go out in his little boat again. He would go out in the morning and come back with the fish at night. He would be safe from the icebergs and the storms.

Her mother smiled.

"He'll be safe," she said. "If we love him, he'll be safe wherever he goes."

One night, when Lucy was dreaming of the sea inside herself, a great ship moved among the islands. The lighthouse beam turned and turned, bringing the ship safely home.

In the daylight, her mother called her.

"Lucy! Lucy! Lucy!"

Lucy rubbed her eyes. She went downstairs. She saw her dad coming through the door and reaching out to her.

He held her tight. He smiled and smiled. He smelt of sea and salt and fish as big as men.

"And look!" he said. "Look what came up in the net."

He held the white pebble shaped like a girl in his hand.

"Another one," he said. "Just like you!"

Lucy smiled and closed her eyes.

He put the pebble in her hand.

"It's Lucy Three!" he said.

Lucy laughed and laughed. She licked the pebble and tasted the salt from the sea. She thought of the boy with scaly skin and seabird fingers, the boy who swims forever and forever, the boy who would come back to her in the deepest night.

"No," she said. She held him tight. "Just Lucy Two, come home again with you."

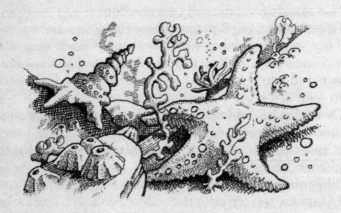

Motorway Dog
Philippa Pearce

At last Elly was going to be allowed to have a dog.

"Only if you really look after it – "

"No incessant barking – "

"No muddy footprints all over the floor – "

To make sure, Elly's parents chose the dog. They left Elly and her younger brother, Matthew, behind when they went to a Home for abandoned dogs. They came back with a brown-and-white splodged dog, small-to-medium-sized, short-haired, stocky.

"Not a bitch," said their father. Their mother gave a slight shudder. "A mongrel, of course," he added.

"Cross-bred," corrected their mother, who cared what the neighbours thought.

While they talked, Elly was holding the dog in her arms and Matthew was trying to pat and stroke it. The dog looked aloofly over the little boy's head. After a while Matthew tired, and went back to his cars and trains. Elly held the dog closer, burying her face in its coat, whispering into its ear, "Dog… Dog… What shall we call you? Have you a name already? Tell me, tell me."

Her father was saying, "The Home couldn't say how old. Couldn't say much at all. Found lost and hungry by a motorway. The usual story: unwanted dog, dump it on a motorway…"

"Why a motorway?" asked Elly. Then, "Oh, I see! How horrible!" She hugged the dog even closer, so that it struggled to be free.

The dog learnt quickly the important things to do and not to do indoors – or perhaps he

67

knew them already. He was given a collar with his address and telephone number on a tag, and his new name: Bob. This name was after a favourite uncle – the very one who had suggested getting a dog from a Dog's Home. "It would be a kindness to a homeless dog," their Uncle Bob had said.

Yet this dog did not gracefully accept his name and settle down, as everyone had expected he would. He seemed almost to hold himself apart from his new family, and he seldom bothered to come when he was called. Elly worried about that. She coaxed him, "Bob...Bob... What's wrong with that for a name? What other name would you have liked? Just tell me. Only tell me." She brought her face beseechingly close to the dog's, but the dog turned his head away, as if embarrassed.

The dog seemed happiest – or at least most at ease – when he went in the car. He was made to sit between Elly and Matthew on the back seat, where they talked to him.

The family took him with them one sunny Saturday on a day trip to the sea. The weather was so hot that they took swimming things and a picnic to the beach; and, when they parked the car, they decided they must leave the doors open to let the air in. There was debate about this but, after all, the car would always be in view, and there were few people about, anyway.

Meanwhile, the dog went with the children down to the very edge of the sea. Plainly he had never seen such a thing before: he was amazed, and also suspicious. He barked at the waves as they curved over and broke before him, and he snarled at the sheet of water that afterwards slid towards him, threatening to wet his paws. He scuttled backwards away from its attack.

He preferred the sand-dunes, where he wandered far and wide.

And then they lost him.

He had been with them for the picnic lunch, of course, on the off-chance of scraps. After lunch Elly and Matthew played, while their parents dozed in the sun. Nobody paid attention when the dog sauntered off amongst the dunes. But when they began to collect all their picnic and other things, in order to take them back to the car, the dog was missing.

They called him again and again; he did not come.

They spread out and searched the dunes, calling constantly: "Bob...Bob...Bob..." Elly was becoming desperate and Matthew was crying – he was tired out anyway.

At last their mother said, "It's no good. We can't go on looking forever. The dog's gone."

And their father said, "We must pack the car and go home without it. There's nothing more to be done."

Elly wailed.

Her father added, "We'll call at the nearest police station as we go home, and tell them we've lost a dog, and leave details, and then, if he turns up – "

But at the word 'if', Elly collapsed into grief. So, without any help at all, her parents had to load themselves up with all the family belongings and trudge with them to the car, the children trailing behind.

And, when they reached the car, there was the dog curled up in the front passenger seat, waiting for them.

Elly and Matthew were overjoyed, of course. Their parents were exasperated – their father to the point of anger, "So the dog was here all the time, listening to us wearing our voices out shouting for it! Sniggering at us making fools of ourselves, I suppose!"

Elly tried to defend the dog. "He didn't *know* we were calling for him. He – "

Her father interrupted, "That dog should have known. It has a name, and we called that name – called until we were hoarse."

Privately, Elly thought, we *gave* him a name, but he didn't want it. It was the wrong name. If only we knew his old name, his real name...

But Elly said nothing, because she knew it would be useless.

Their father drove them home, fuming most of the way. And it seemed as if he could not forgive the dog for that afternoon's experience. He was on the watch for any more bad behaviour from the dog.

There was always something to complain about.

The dog strayed. Tied up outside a shop, he gnawed his way through his leather lead and went off. They got him back, but only after searches and telephone calls. To their father's fury ("I'm not made of expensive leather leads!") the dog did it a second time. Then he was put on a chain. This time he managed to slip the collar, and was away overnight. He came back in the end, but unmistakably only because there was nowhere else to go.

Once the dog made a scene – almost a scandal – in a super-market car park. Their mother had taken the children with her to do the household shopping and, to keep the children happy, had taken the dog as well. They left Bob in the car, of course, dozing in his favourite spot, the front passenger seat.

They were coming back from their shopping when they heard the muffled uproar of a dog barking. The uproar died as they hurried to the car. They found a small crowd gathered around it, and a little girl crying bitterly. The girl's mother was angry on her behalf, "She just tapped on the window to say hello to the doggy – just tapped on the window, that's all, and all hell broke loose. Rampaging round the inside of the car, barking and snarling and *screaming*, and its jaws snapping. Murderous. That's what it was. Terrifying. You've a dangerous animal in there, you know. I would never trust it."

Elly and Matthew pressed close to their mother and hoped that she would speak up for Bob. She did, "And how was the dog to know that you weren't going to break into the car, like thieves? The dog's got to defend its own home, hasn't it?"

"Home!" said the angry woman. "It's only a dog in a car, for heaven's sake! And it managed to terrify my little girl out of her mind!"

While they argued, the dog sat quietly in the front passenger seat, his body facing forward, but his head turned to watch. Every so often his body quivered and he growled under his breath.

By now the little girl had stopped crying, and the little girl's mother, still indignant, led her away.

"Thanks, Mum," Elly whispered.

"Mind you," said her mother, "it never does bark like that when it's at home. Not when the postman comes, not when visitors ring at the door. So what got into it in the car?"

This mystery worried the children's mother; it continued to do so. She did not believe that Bob was a 'dangerous animal', not to be trusted with Elly and little Matthew. She had seen his patience with them, his long-suffering.

But, all the same, there was *something*…

Did their mother tell their father the story of the supermarket car park? Elly thought probably not. But, anyway, by now their father's complaining about the dog had settled into something ominous, frightening. He declared that the dog was 'not a success', and began to hint that they might as well return it to the Home.

Elly said nothing, but late at night, when everyone else was asleep and she could not sleep, she crept downstairs to the dog in his basket. He woke, but did not greet her. She knelt and put her arms around him: "Please," Elly urged in a whisper, "please be a success…please…please…please…"

The dog only shifted about, trying to move out of her embrace.

Quietly, Elly wept.

Soon after that hopeless night, there was a family expedition to visit their Uncle Bob. The day was sultry, with a thunderstorm threatening. Uncle Bob gave them all a good lunch, with ice cream at the end of it. After lunch, the grown-ups sat in the shade indoors, talking, with Uncle Bob's faithful old spaniel dozing at his master's feet.

The children played in the garden in the paddling pool, which Uncle Bob always had ready in hot weather.

And between the two groups sat the dog called Bob, interested in neither. He had already explored the garden. It was tightly fenced in: not a place to escape from.

For this visit, and rather unusually, the paddling pool had been put right at the bottom of the garden, at the furthest distance from the house. There – Elly realized – it was out of earshot of the conversation indoors. The talkers indoors did not want to be overheard, that was it; and she could guess what they were discussing: the dog – her dog, and what should be done about such an unsatisfactory pet.

But nothing was said openly about the dog either then or afterwards when the family was driving home. Yet nothing else was spoken of either. Silence filled the car, as thundery as the air outside.

They had already joined the traffic on the motorway when Matthew began singing a little song about going to the toilet. His father told him to stop at once; it was distracting. Elly pointed out that Matthew was singing that he *needed* to go to the toilet. Their father became angry that Matthew had not gone at Uncle Bob's, when he'd been told to. Matthew said that he'd only been *asked* to go to the toilet, and he'd said, 'No, thank you'. Elly began explaining that Matthew hadn't understood the difference between being asked and being told, and her father now became very irritated, and their mother interrupted to say that they must stop at the very next Service Station or there might be an accident in the car.

Luckily there was a Service Station soon. They moved off the lanes of the motorway into the Service Area, behind a caravan and several other cars and lorries and huge heavy goods vehicles. They found the parking for Cars Only and parked, and then began to argue. Matthew said that he didn't need the toilet after all, and his mother said he must go, anyway – and hurry, because it might begin raining at any moment. Their father said he needed to get out to stretch his legs and breathe some fresh air; and Elly said that she would stay in the car with the dog. Her mother didn't like that arrangement, so Elly would have to go with her father. That would have left the dog alone in the car, and the children's mother liked that arrangement even less.

In the end they all got out, and their mother said they might as well all have some tea, after Matthew's toilet visit. They couldn't go inside because of the dog, so they settled on a table and chairs outside, hoping the rain would hold off long enough for tea. They piled all their waterproofs on the back of the chair with most room to spare, which was Matthew's, of course, and also hung his little pink umbrella there.

Elly sat, looking at her dog. Her father had slipped the loop of the dog-chain under one of the legs of his chair, and his own weight as he sat on the chair would hold the chair leg on the ground and hold the dog's chain and the dog its prisoner. Elly noticed how the dog watched everybody coming and going, and listened to everything. There were car noises of every kind, and people's voices talking, and children calling in some game, and a baby screaming, and the far-away tail-end of some kind of whistling that made the dog sit up and quiver in attention. But he made no attempt to get away; he know he could not.

Now Matthew's mother was insisting on his visit to the toilet. The little boy began getting off his chair rather clumsily, and the chair began to fall backwards with the weight of the waterproofs. Their father saw what was happening and lunged forward to stop it, but the pink umbrella swung out and hit him on the head – not hard, but hard enough for him to lose his balance and his own chair slipped from under him, all four chair-legs in the air for a second as he fell, shouting something that his family could not at first understand.

Then, "The dog – the dog!" he was shouting as he picked himself up from a muddle of waterproofs and a pink umbrella. "The dog's GONE!"

So he had, in a flash, with his chain flying behind him like a paper streamer. He vanished through the legs of all the people.

Their father was beside himself with rage; their mother was calmer, worrying only about Matthew and his needs. The two of them went off together: they would be back at the tea table as soon as they could. And perhaps the dog would have come back of its own accord by then.

Perhaps; but Elly thought not, and she could see that her father was certain not. He wanted to set off at once in pursuit, but looked at Elly and the heap of waterproofs and the pink umbrella piled back on their chair, and did not know what to do.

Elly said, "I'm old enough. I'll stay here and guard them. I'll be all right. I won't move from here. I promise."

Her father said fiercely, "You're not to budge an inch. You're not to speak to anybody either. Understand?"

Elly said, "Yes."

She sat at the table wondering what would happen, and the sun came out unexpectedly from behind the clouds and shone in her face, dazzling her. She looked down, and then – conscious of a shadow falling on her – looked up again and faced a man who seemed a giant against the light of the setting sun. He was wearing a donkey-jacket which he held against his chest. From between the front folds of the jacket a pair of eyes looked down at her intelligently.

Startled into speech, she said, "You've got our dog!"

"No," said the man. "Mine." And Elly, staring, saw that they belonged together – a dog and his master. "I lost him," said the man. "Now I buy him back. I want everything to be legal." With his free hand the man was reaching into a pocket. He said: "I saw him with your Pa. Your Pa wouldn't easy have given him up."

"No," said Elly.

"But then he got loose, and he came to me."

"You called him," said Elly.

"Yes."

"What's his name, then?"

"His name?"

The big man paused in what he was doing, taken aback. "He hasn't a name," he said. Then he reconsidered, "Well, I do call him Matey. Or Partner. Or Mister Dog. Or just Mister."

"But when you want him to come to you – I mean, from far away."

"Oh that," said the man. "I whistle."

He pursed his lips; he whistled.

Then Elly recognized the tail-end of a whistling that she had heard earlier that afternoon; and the dog nestling against his master's breast knew the sound, too. He poked his head forward to look up enquiringly into the face above him.

The whistle lasted only for seconds, yet it lingered on the ear like bird-song heard in sleep. It had a question in it ('Where are you? Where?') and an entreaty ('Come to me – oh come!'), and in every note was the enticement of tenderness.

The whistling had ended, but Elly still listened.

Meanwhile the man was bringing out from his pocket a handful of money. He said, "After this we're off. Back on the road."

"The road?" said Elly. "Is it a heavy goods vehicle?" But she saw that this must be what he drove.

"HGV. That's it," said the man. "You need a mate for that." He made a sound that might have been a laugh. "A mate with a bark and a bite. With a snarl and a snap."

Even while he spoke, he had been sorting out on to the table a little pile of notes. "All's to be legal," he said.

"No!" cried Elly, waking up to what he was doing. "No need!" As she spoke, she was trying to stop bank notes sliding and blowing away. "No need!" But when she looked up from the money, the big man was gone.

And then came her father huffing and puffing up to her with his questions, "Who was he? What did he want: Why were you talking to him, when I told you – I *told* you – "

Elly interrupted him, "It was Bob. He took Bob."

Her father saw the pile of notes on the table, "You *sold* Bob! You sold your own dog!"

"No," said Elly. "He was his dog. He'd lost him. He left us money for him. Just to be legal."

Her father was counting the money and exclaiming in amazement at the amount, "The creature wasn't worth all this!"

And now the other two had arrived back from their trip to the toilet, and what had been happening must be explained to them. Elly found that difficult: something had happened, but it seemed so unlikely. Yet it had happened.

The disappearance of the dog changed all plans. They were not going to bother about tea, after all. They would go straight home. On the way home the children's father was in an unusually good mood. He said over and over again that, with all this cash, they could buy what he called 'a proper dog' from a breeder; and it would be a puppy. (Matthew was delighted at the prospect.) After all, that was what Uncle Bob now advised. ('So that was what they were plotting this afternoon,' thought Elly.)

Elly did not join in the talk. She was thinking her own thoughts; and she was also on the look-out for any HGV on the motorway – as she would be for a long time to come. She was not sure that she would be able to recognize the driver, but she was certain of his mate on the front passenger seat. He would be sitting on some kind of cushion, to bring him up to eye-level for the windscreen and the side-windows.

She was glad for him to be there, where he belonged; and yet… Suddenly she was angry that he had been taken from her: after all, he was *her* dog.

But no, not really hers. Never hers. In her heart she knew.

So – yes, she would be glad some day to see him there, sitting on his cushion, sharp-eyed, alert, ready to guard his master and his master's property with snarl and snap: Mister Dog.

The Wrong Eye
Anthony Horowitz

The Director General of the BBC was a big man with a big desk, but he was in big trouble and he was sweating. He drew a tissue across the gleaming dome of his forehead. It had turned to mush before it got halfway. His face was the colour of damp cheese and if he tugged at his beard much more, it was going to wave goodbye to his chin. He looked like a man who had just managed to mislay twenty-six million pounds of somebody else's money – which wasn't surprising, because he had.

THE BUCK STOPS HERE

His name was Dick Gregson. I could see the two initials – DG – on the pocket of his shirt. Or maybe they stood for Director General. Or maybe even Dreadfully Grey. He was that, too. He wasn't alone in the room. There were two men and a woman on his side of the desk and sitting opposite them, next to me, my big brother – Tim Diamond.

Gregson needed a private detective. I don't know how he'd come across Tim, but one thing I was certain about. Tim Diamond was the worst private detective in the country, if not the world. I was only thirteen years old but without me he'd never have caught a crook in his life. Without me, he'd have trouble catching a bus. Maybe Gregson had found Tim in The Yellow Pages. If so, he must have been looking in the section marked 'Complete Idiots'.

"It goes without saying," Gregson rasped, "that this is an extremely delicate business."

Tim half-closed one eye. "If it goes without saying," he asked "why did you just say it?"

"Well…" Gregson blinked. "It was a figure of speech…"

"OK, DG. So let's have a little speech about figures. And the figure of twenty-six million is the one I've got in mind."

Gregson nodded. "The whole thing is madness," he said. "Total madness. Twenty-six million pounds…the amount that we raised for this year's BBC Children in Need Appeal. And now it's gone. All of it!"

"These children," Tim asked. "Whose children are they?"

"Well…everyone's! It's a charity, Mr Diamond. We help children all over the UK."

"I see, DG…" Tim leant back in his chair and crossed his legs. His foot caught the edge of the coffee table, shattering the glass. Tim looked down at the network of cracks that had, only a moment ago, been the Director General's favourite piece of furniture. "Why don't you start at the beginning?" he said.

"Very well." I could see that Gregson was beginning to wonder just what it was that had walked into his life. But it was too late to back out now. "This year we managed to raise more than ever before," he said. "We were all very proud of ourselves. And that was when Guy had his big idea."

He glanced at the man sitting nearest to him, and I somehow knew that Guy's career had just taken a nose-dive. Guy Malone was about forty years old. His hair had turned grey and so, for that matter, had his skin, his eyes and the rest of him. I suppose that's what comes from working too long at the BBC. Guy looked like he had just come back from a funeral. From the way he was sitting there, it could have been his own.

"Guy is a producer," Gregson went on. "He's produced variety shows, magic shows and comedy shows. But right now he's the producer of the BBC's most popular children's show – *Blue Cheetah*."

"Oh yes!" Tim exclaimed. "I watch it all the time!" He blushed. "I mean...I used to. When I was a kid."

That wasn't true. Tim still watched *Blue Cheetah* every afternoon. Inspired by the programme, he'd once collected two thousand yoghurt cartons for the local hospital. Curiously enough, after eating two thousand yoghurts, that was exactly where he'd ended up. He'd also built a tree house out of Fairy Liquid bottles. It was just a shame we didn't have a tree.

"Guy's idea was to show all the money that we'd raised on *Blue Cheetah*," Gregson explained. "To let people see it."

"It was to show everyone how generous they'd been," Guy cut in. "We'd actually have twenty-six million pounds in the studio! In fifty pound notes..."

"That's right," Gregson didn't sound amused. "So that's what we did. We took twenty-six million pounds out of the bank and showed it to the studio audience...and to the millions watching at home. Andy Harris, our head of security, was in charge of the money. And Melissa Tweed, as usual, was the presenter.

Harris was the other man in the room. He was dark, thick-set, built like a horse and with teeth to match. He'd been in the army and it showed. He had short hair, muscles and a map of Bosnia tattooed on his neck. I'd recognized Melissa Tweed the moment I came into the room. She was blonde and bubbly and never stopped smiling. Melissa obviously thought she was still on TV. Five minutes with her and I was looking for the off switch.

"It was a lovely, lovely idea," she burbled now. "It's just a shame it went a teeny bit wrong."

"A teeny bit wrong?" the Director General yelled. "We lost the money! All of it!"

"Oh yes!" Melissa giggled.

"Wait a minute," Tim drawled, "you say you lost the money. Have you tried looking behind the cushions of the sofa?"

I half-closed my eyes.

The Director General stared at Tim. "I'm talking about twenty-six million pounds, you nit-wit!" he screamed. "Not my loose change!"

"Why don't you tell us what happened?" I suggested.

Gregson looked at me as if seeing me for the first time. "Who are you?" he demanded.

It was nice of him to notice me. "My name is Nick Diamond," I said. "I'm his brother."

"Shouldn't you be at school?"

"School can manage without me. Just tell us what happened."

Gregson considered. "I can do better than that," he said. "I can show you."

There was a television and video player in the corner of the room. He picked up a remote control and turned it on. Tim settled back in his chair, And together we watched the impossible theft. It happened right in front of our eyes.

There was the *Blue Cheetah* set. Melissa was on the screen, pointing at a great pile of money sitting in the back of an orange and white security truck parked just behind her. "...and we're going to help hundreds and hundreds of children," she was saying. "And it's all thanks to you!" She gave a little squeal of surprise. "And look who's here!" she exclaimed. "It's Pudsey Bear!"

As the audience applauded, a man walked onto the stage, dressed in a yellow, furry bear suit with a patch over his eye. He raised his hand and waved.

"Who's the man dressed up as Slugsy?" Tim asked.

"That's me," Harris replied. The Head of Security watched himself on the small screen. "I wanted to stay close to the money the whole time it was in the studio...and until it was returned to the bank. I figured dressing up as Pudsey was the best way to do it."

The camera closed in on the money mountain. The truck was about five metres high and twenty metres long and the whole thing was completely stuffed with banknotes. I had to admit that Guy Malone was right. It was amazing to see how much cash had been raised. The audience was cheering now as Pudsey – or Harris – walked round the back, momentarily disappearing from sight. But then he was back again, closing the doors and climbing into the driving seat. It seemed that he was going to drive the truck off himself.

"So let's wave goodbye to Pudsey!" Melissa trilled. "He's off to the bank with the money. I suppose it must be Bear-clays Bank!" The audience laughed. So did Melissa, watching herself on TV. The engine of the truck started up. Part of the set was lifted up on ropes and a great cloud of smoke rolled in.

"My God!" Tim yelled. "The studio's on fire!"

"No," Guy told him. "It's a special effect. It's dry ice. It was meant to make the whole thing more dramatic."

"What's on the other side of the smoke?" I asked.

"There's a second, smaller studio with an exit out onto the street," Guy said. "It was completely empty. Nobody was allowed in there until the money had gone."

"And where did it go?"

"You can see for yourself," Harris said. "The truck was filmed by one of the BBC's security cameras."

The second part of the film was grainy, black and white. An electric door on the side of the BBC opened and the truck rolled out. It had taken less than five seconds to travel from the *Blue Cheetah* studio, through the smaller studio, and out onto the street. Pudsey Bear was still driving. But now he was joined by four waiting police cars that accompanied him, two in the front, two at the back, as he drove away from the building.

"I didn't stop the truck once," Harris continued. "I went out of the studio and the police followed me all the way to the bank. Exactly as we'd planned."

"Except, when the truck finally got to the bank, it was empty!" Gregson exploded. "You've seen for yourself. It was full in the studio, it drove out of the studio without stopping. Four police cars met it. It went – without stopping – to the bank. Andy Harris was behind the wheel the whole time. He took off the bear suit when he got to the bank. Then he opened the door…"

"…and all the money had gone," Harris finished. "There wasn't a single note in the truck. Not a penny!"

"Could it have fallen out on the way?" Tim asked.

"It was locked in! In a high security van! The police were there! Of course it didn't fall out!" Gregson wrenched at his beard and another chunk came out in his hand.

"I only asked," Tim said

"Let's take a look at the studio," I suggested. If he suffered any more stress, I was afraid it was going to be DG RIP.

Melissa took us down. It was strange to walk through the *Blue Cheetah* studio. There was no audience there now and the cameras were standing idle, blind witnesses to the empty stage.

"That's where the truck went..." she said.

The walls looked solid but of course they were all made of wood and fabric so they could be moved easily. We went through the exit and into the next studio, which clearly hadn't been used for a while. There were no cameras here. The far wall seemed to be made of brick. To one side was an electric roll-up door; the sort of thing you might find on a garage, only bigger. It was this door that had opened to allow the truck out.

"This is the small studio," Melissa told us. She grinned. "It's even smaller than I remember. The truck came through here and that was the last I saw of it."

"The studio was empty when the truck came through?" I asked, remembering what Malone had said.

"Yes. That's right," Melissa nodded. "Nobody was allowed anywhere near. Mr Harris insisted. He said it would be more secure."

Dick Gregson had followed us down. "You have to find the money," he said. And suddenly there were tears in his eyes. "We've come to you, Mr Diamond, because we can't go to the police. If the public found out what had happened... we'd be destroyed! Can you imagine what the papers would say? They're horrible enough about our programmes. But this...! We have to get the money back. And we have to do it quickly."

"This business may look dodgy, DG," Tim said, "but you have my word. I won't rest until I've found the money."

In fact, he fell asleep on the bus home. As usual, if anyone was going to solve this mystery it was going to have to be me.

*

It was early evening by the time we got home. Ever since my parents had unexpectedly emigrated to Australia, Tim and I had been sharing a small flat in Camden Town. There was a glass door with TIM DIAMOND PRIVATE DETECTIVE written on the front. It led into an office with a view of Camden Market. There was more of our furniture in the market than there was in the flat. Tim had sold it to pay the rent. It was funny really. Looking out of the window I felt more at home than when I turned around and looked at the home.

Fortunately, we still had a video and TV. Dick Gregson had given us a copy of the video and, while Tim opened a tin of beans in the kitchen, I played it a couple more times. It still seemed impossible that anyone could have taken the money. There it was in the back of the truck. Andy Harris, dressed as Pudsey Bear, got in. The truck drove off. It never stopped. And yet when it arrived at the bank...

"How do you want your beans?" Tim called out.

"Baked!" I replied.

"There's some cheese in the fridge!"

"That's not cheese, Tim. That's mould..."

Tim came into the room. At the same time, I reached out and pressed the PAUSE button. "That's funny," I said.

"There's nothing funny about mould," Tim replied. "It's very unhygienic."

"I'm not talking about mould. I'm talking about this." I pointed at the screen. "Look at Pudsey's eye-patch."

Tim leant forward. You probably know Pudsey Bear well enough...a big yellow bear with two buttons sewn into his stomach. I've often wondered about the buttons. Why have buttons when you don't actually have clothes? But that wasn't what I was looking at now. As usual, Pudsey was wearing an eye-patch, a red and white spotted handkerchief. But it was over his left eye.

"It's the wrong eye," I said.

"What do you mean?" Tim asked.

"Pudsey always wears a handkerchief over his right eye. The other eye. I'm sure of it."

"But that's not the *real* Pudsey Bear," Tim said. "It's the Head of Security dressed up as Pudsey Bear."

I ignored him and span the tape back on fast rewind. I reached the point where Harris was waving to the audience, just before he disappeared round the back of the truck. And there it was! In this shot, the handkerchief was on the right eye. I pointed this out.

"He must have moved the handkerchief as he walked round the truck," Tim said.

"Why would he do that?"

"Maybe it fell off..."

"I don't think so, Tim."

And suddenly I knew everything. Maybe you know the feeling when you're doing a puzzle or watching a whodunit on television, and it all comes together in an instant. That was what it was like. I remember Gregson taking about the *Blue Cheetah* producer...

"*He's produced variety shows, magic shows and comedy shows...*"

And there was something else. Melissa showing us round the *Blue Cheetah* studio. I remembered how one wall of the set had been lifted up to allow us to pass through. And what was it she had said to us while we were in the second, smaller studio?

"Forget the beans, Tim!" I said.

"What beans?" Tim asked.

"I think I know where the money is. We're going out."

"Where?"

"Back to the BBC!"

*

It was dark by the time we arrived back at the BBC Television Centre. Tim had been given a security pass and the man at the gate didn't try to stop us as we went in. There were quite a few well-known faces in the reception area: footballers, pop stars and actors. Tim didn't recognize any of them but he got a nice autograph from the receptionist. We made our way down a passage, heading for the *Blue Cheetah* studio. But that wasn't what interested me. I went straight across the stage and into the smaller studio next door. There were no windows here and barely any light. I knew what I was looking for but I wasn't quite sure how to find it.

"What are we doing here?" Tim whispered.

"We're looking for the money," I told him.

"But Nick! The money's been stolen!"

"This way!" I said.

There was a ladder leading up to a steel platform that ran round the entire studio, about ten metres above the ground.

This is where the lights hung when the studio was being used. I pushed Tim ahead of me and we climbed up. We had just reached the top when there was the sound of a door opening and voices...two men talking. It was impossible to see through the gloom but I knew I'd heard those voices before. I realized we had just arrived in time.

There was silence. Then the clunk of a car door opening and closing. Tim had heard it too. He turned to me – puzzled. There was no car in the studio. The whole place was empty. Even the two men were out of sight. So what had he just heard? I raised a finger to my lips.

And then somebody must have pressed a button because there was an electronic whirr and the roll-up door leading onto the street began to open. This was the door that the security truck had taken on its way to meet the police escort. At the same time, I became aware that something else was moving on the far side of the room. An entire wall was being raised...just like the wall in the *Blue Cheetah* studio.

There was an orange and white truck parked behind it. It was exactly the same as the truck that had taken the money.

"Nick...!" Tim hissed. "Why has the truck come back?"

"It hasn't come back," I replied. "It never left!"

"But we saw it...on the video."

"That was a different truck!"

There was a roar as the engine of this truck started up and it backed out. It was going to drive away and there was nothing I could do to sop it. Everything was happening too quickly.

"This way!" I shouted. There was no way either of the two men would hear me above the noise of the engine.

I followed the metal gantry round. It went over the top of the roll-up door so that I could look straight down onto the roof of the truck as it drove through. Tim knew what I was going to do.

"You're not...!" he began.

"I am!" I said.

And jumped.

I landed like a cat on the top of the roof. That would have been fine. Unfortunately, Tim had decided to follow me. And he had landed more like a hippopotamus. The two men inside the truck would have felt the crash even if they hadn't heard it. And now they knew they had an extra passenger. The driver must have stamped his foot down on the accelerator because the truck surged forward almost throwing me off the roof. Then it burst through the security barrier and swerved out onto the main road, heading for the motorway.

There were no handholds on the roof the truck. I was lying flat on my stomach with my legs splayed, the cold metal pressed against my face. I saw Tim rolling to one side and yelled out to him.

"Grab onto something!"

I winced as his fingers hooked into my leg.

"Not me!" I yelled.

The driver wrenched the wheel a second time, spinning across the road, trying to shake us off. It was a cold night and the wind rushed into us, trying to swat us as if we were two human flies. The truck was on the wrong side of the road now and there was the blast of a horn as a car, coming the other way, threatened to crash into it in a head-on collision. The driver swerved back onto the right side and Tim and I were once again sent sprawling. I saw Tim jack-knife over the edge of the truck and threw myself forward, catching hold of his ankles at the last minute. We must have been doing about seventy miles per hour. Now I heard something else. The wail of a police siren! It was the best sound I'd heard all night.

But the driver wasn't giving up yet. He had reached the ramp that led up to the M40 motorway and now he was going even faster. I had to use all my strength to keep hold of Tim. Only his feet were showing. His body was suspended below and I could hear the thudding as it swung out and back into the side of the truck. He was going to have a bad headache the next day. If he still had a head.

And then the inevitable happened. The driver lost control. Suddenly the truck was spinning in an impossible circle. I lost sight of everything. The motorway, the streetlamps, the traffic and the fast approaching police car became a twisting, shimmering blur. Now I knew what a spider felt like when it was being sucked down the bath. There was a crash and Tim and I were thrown into the air. Perhaps I was imagining it, but I could have sworn I heard him shout "Wheee!" as we hurtled to our deaths.

Except we didn't die. There was a grassy bank beside the motorway and that was where we landed: me on the grass, Tim in a bed of stinging nettles. Meanwhile, the truck had hit the central reservation, bounced back and collided with a concrete bridge. There was a grinding explosion as the metal crumpled and then I was aware that it had begun to rain. Not water. Fifty pound notes.

Twenty-six million pounds of the BBC's money gently fell on us, forming a blanket where we lay.

*

"Once I'd seen it was the wrong eye, the rest was easy," I explained.

Tim and I were in hospital. He was in bed with two sprained ankles and multiple nettle stings. I was visiting. Dick Gregson, the Director General of the BBC was with us. He'd bought Tim a bunch of grapes, which was nice of him. Personally, I'd have preferred a cheque.

"It was Malone's idea," I went on. "I remember you telling me that he had once produced magic shows. Well, that's how he did it. The whole thing was a giant magic trick."

Malone had been pulled out of the truck and arrested. Andy Harris, the head of security, had been with him. Neither man had been hurt in the crash. They'd both be in perfect condition when they began their ten years in jail.

"They performed a double switch," I said. "This is how it works: Harris is dressed up as Pudsey Bear. He walks round the back of the truck but when he disappears from sight, that's when they swap places. And it's Malone who comes round the other side, dressed in a bear costume of his own."

"But with the eye-patch on the wrong eye," Gregson said.

This guy was smart. No wonder he was the head of the BBC.

"Right. Meanwhile, Harris runs into the smaller studio. It's completely empty – he's already made sure of that – and he's got a second, identical orange and white truck hidden there – behind the false wall. That was the other clue. Melissa Tweed said that the studio looked smaller than she remembered. That's because the entire brick wall was fake."

"So Malone drives the truck with the money into the studio, and Harris drives an empty truck out!" Gregson said.

"Exactly. The whole thing only takes five seconds and it looks as if Harris has been driving all the time. But the police cars waiting outside are escorting an empty truck. And as soon as they think it's safe, Harris and Malone come back to pick up the real truck – with all the cash!" I paused. "That was where we came in."

"You've done a great job," Gregson said. "We've got all the money back and nobody need ever know what happened. I'm going to send you both a free television licence and an invitation to *The Weakest Link*…"

"Goodbye," I said.

The Director General left.

Tim looked at me and tried to smile. It wasn't easy. The nettles really had done terrible things to his face. He'd gone almost completely yellow. There were two black bruises on his chest. And one of his eyes had become so swollen the doctors had been forced to cover it with a handkerchief. In fact, for a moment he reminded me of someone, but I must have been tired because I didn't have the faintest idea who.

The Dayspring
Martin Waddell

A stone hero lay in a cathedral, Major Arbuthnot, V.C., surrounded by flags and by drums.

In a stall on the wall above Major Arbuthnot, V.C., were John William Lennox and Maud, carved in wood.

All day the cathedral was busy but, at night, when the people had gone, there was quiet, and peace.

Then, one night, with a roar and a shake, the world B R O K E !

In the mess and the rubble lay John William Lennox and Maud. There was no more of Major Arbuthnot. He'd gone west, with the rest.

"What's all this about then, Johnny?" asked Maud, sitting up.

"Well, I'm bothered," said John William Lennox. "You're *talking*!"

"It's right queer, ain't it?" said Maud. "I thought I was just made of wood!"

"It was good wood," said John William Lennox, "and old!"

"But that doesn't explain you and me talking!" said Maud.

They got up and shook themselves down and looked all about them, at the ruins.

"Is anyone there?" shouted John William Lennox.

"Please help us!" cried Maud.

Nobody came. Nothing stirred. They clung close together in the dirt and the dust, John William Lennox and Maud.

"We're out on our own, lass!" said John William Lennox.

"I don't like it, our Johnny!" said Maud. "What do we think we're about?"

"I haven't a clue, lass," said John William Lennox. "But I think, pretty soon, we'll find out!" They both shouted again, but nobody came.

"Maybe it's *Him*," said John William Lennox, "happen He's made a mistake, and blowed the lot up!"

"I don't think He'd do that!" said Maud. "It was *them*, and their soldiers and guns!"

"Reckon you're right!" said John William Lennox. "But this isn't much to comfort us!"

And then came a G L O W.

"Don't look now, lass!" said John William Lennox. "But there's something up there!"

"What is it?" said Maud.

"I can't rightly tell," said John William Lennox. "But I think it's looking at us!"

And then...a Voice came.

"You awright, lads?" It asked.

"We're rightly!" said John William Lennox.

"Right poorly!" said Maud, "and just a shade battered to boot!"

"Never mind," said the Voice.

"BUT WE DO!" said John William Lennox and Maud, who were feeling...well, odd.

"I thought the old place was in a bit of a mess, lads," said the Voice. "So I thought, 'Better chuck it, and start again!' So I have, and I did, and you're IT! And good luck, 'cause I reckon you'll need it."

Then the glow faded away. They were left in the dust, feeling dazed.

"Who was that, lass?" whispered John William Lennox.

"It was *Him*," said Maud, "Him up *There*, like, imagine *Him* picking on us."

"But *why* us, lass?" asked John William Lennox.

"Why not us?" said Maud.

"Because we're made of wood!" said John William Lennox. "Though it is good wood, and old!"

"Reckon he trusts us," said Maud. "He's trusting us to trust Him!"

"That's not much of an answer!" said John William Lennox.

"It is all that you're getting!" said Maud.

"Well then, we'd better get started," said John William Lennox, "though I don't rightly know how to start!"

"Get digging and planting!" said Maud.

And they did.

They did what they could, the two bits of wood, digging and planting, but it takes a long time making a world without soldiers and guns and Cathedrals and flags.

But they did what they could...John William Lennox and Maud.

The Dreamcatcher
Malorie Blackman

Katy started work on her dreamcatcher on Tuesday afternoon. For three days and well into the evening, Katy worked on her dreamcatcher. Even when she was so tired she could hardly keep her eyes open or her head up, she forced herself to carry on. And just before she got into bed, she set her alarm for 6.30am. The alarm clock had been a sixth birthday present from her Aunt Edie – but Dad hated it. He said it was loud enough to wake the dead. That was why Katy liked it. Each night she put it under her pillow so that its ringing would wake her up, but not disturb her dad. She couldn't let him know what she was up to because he wouldn't like it. He would stop her from finishing her dreamcatcher and Katy couldn't let that happen.

She had to finish it before her ninth birthday on Sunday. JC at school said dreamcatchers didn't work once you were nine or over. Everyone, including Katy had laughed at the idea. A dreamcatcher! How ridiculous was that! Except that, inside, Katy wasn't laughing at all. Inside, Katy had listened to each and every word. Suppose, just suppose, JC was right. Suppose it was possible to make dreamcatchers just the way he said, to catch dreams and a lot more besides. Katy made up her mind in that moment to give it a try. But she only had a few days left. If she didn't catch her dream before her birthday, she'd never catch the one dream she wanted. The only dream she was after. So she worked harder and longer on her dreamcatcher than she'd ever worked on anything before.

And it was worth it. The dreamcatcher was astonishing.

Katy used an old wire hanger to make her tennis-racket shaped frame. She wound cotton wool strips, then her mum's favourite silk scarf around the short handle to cover the sharp edges of metal. The scarf was held in place with a number of multi-coloured elastic bands. On the circular frame she looped row upon row of wool from one of her mum's favourite jumpers. It was a sunshine yellow jumper that her mum didn't wear any more. Better to use it in the dreamcatcher than let it collect dust in the wardrobe. To decorate the frame, Katy used chopped up bits of old photographs buried deep in the multitude of albums Dad kept concealed at the back of one of the bookcases.

Three long days it took. But at last it was ready. And not before time, too. It was Thursday evening and Katy had only two nights before her birthday to catch the dream she so desperately wanted. She was dog tired and ready to go to sleep right there and then, but she had to wait. Wait until she'd eaten her dinner. Wait until she'd had her bath and cleaned her teeth. Wait until she'd put on her pyjamas and got into bed.

"What story would you like tonight, princess?" asked Dad.

"No story tonight, Dad," Katy shook her head.

"No story!" Dad placed a concerned hand on Katy's forehead. "Are you feeling all right?"

"I'm fine," Katy's eyelids fluttered and she forced them to open.

"Not even a short one?"

"No thanks, Dad. I'm a bit tired." Which was nothing but the truth.

"You're not coming down with something, are you?"

"No," Katy forced a smile. "Just tired."

"OK. Goodnight, princess." Dad bent to kiss Katy's forehead. "Sweet dreams."

Dad walked across the room and switched off the light. Katy closed her eyes, pretending to be asleep already.

"Goodnight," Dad sighed.

He shut the door as he left the room. Katy waited until she heard the sound of his footsteps going downstairs before opening her eyes. She stared into the darkness, her eyes wide open, her breath held somewhere in her throat. Only when the sound of footsteps had died out completely did Katy exhale softly. She was afraid that the very noise would alert Dad to the fact that she wasn't as ready to go to sleep as she'd pretended. Yes, she was tired but there were still things to do. Katy threw back the covers and padded across the carpet to her window. She pulled back one of the curtains, staring in surprise at the full moon, as bright as a new coin in the purple-black night sky overflowing with stars. Katy stood on tiptoe and opened her window wide, taking care not to lean out too far. Cold, winter air rushed in to meet her, its sharpness taking her breath away. Katy was tempted to shut the window at once, but she didn't. She thought that the dreams she wanted would find their way into her room anyway, but she wanted to make it easier for them. She had to be sure that they would reach her.

Katy tiptoed back to her bed and felt under it for her dreamcatcher. Running her hand along the soft carpet, she shivered as the cold night air swirled around her. Already the temperature in the room was dropping. Katy found her dreamcatcher and hopped into bed, pulling the covers up to her chin. She placed the dreamcatcher on her chest, next to her heart.

"Dreamcatcher," Katy whispered. "Please send me the dream I want before my birthday."

That was what scared Katy most of all. Her ninth birthday was so close. And if she didn't receive the dream she wanted by then, it would never come true. JC had said so. But she couldn't think like that. It would work. It *had* to. It was time to put her dreamcatcher to the test. Katy closed her eyes – and before a minute had passed, she was fast asleep, her arms crossed over her dreamcatcher, hugging it to her.

"Katy? Wake up, Katy. What's that you're holding? And is that my favourite scarf I can see tied around it?"

Katy opened her eyes slowly. Her curtains were open and summer sunlight poured into every nook and cranny of the room. And there, perched on the edge of her bed sat her mum.

"Hi, Mum," Katy's smile was pure happiness.

"Hi, sleepy head," Mum smiled back. "How are you feeling?"

"Good. Brilliant. I had the best dream…"

"I'm glad," said Mum. "But d'you mind telling me what you're doing with my scarf? By the time you've finished, it's going to look like a dog's been chewing it."

"I thought you wouldn't mind if I borrowed it," admitted Katy. "I also borrowed a bit of your yellow jumper."

"Why?"

Katy held up her invention. "To make this. A dreamcatcher."

"Oh." Mum considered the thing in Katy's hand. "Did it work?"

"I don't know yet," Katy said, slowly.

"What dream were you trying to catch?"

"I can't tell you," Katy's smile faded.

"Why not?" asked Mum.

"I'm afraid it won't work if I tell you."

"I see. Then by all means you must keep it to yourself," said Mum. "Any chance of getting my scarf back?"

"Can I hold on to it? Just for a couple of days? Just until my birthday?" Katy pleaded.

"I don't know…"

But Katy could see from the twinkle in Mum's eyes that she wasn't going to make Katy hand it back.

"Thanks, Mum." Katy sat up happily.

"Isn't it a beautiful day." Mum stood up and walked over to the window. The streaming sunlight lit her ebony hair, tinting it a million shades of autumn brown. Katy jumped out of bed and ran over to her mum, slipping her cool hand inside Mum's warm one.

"I've missed you, Mum," said Katy.

"I know." Mum smiled down at her. "But I'm here now."

"For good?"

"Always and forever. I'll always be with you, angel. Even when I'm far away from you, I'll still be with you. D'you understand?"

Katy immediately shook her head. It sounded like one of those baffling things grown-ups said to make you feel better – but which didn't.

"So are you back for good?" Katy repeated urgently.

"No." The word came out as a sigh.

Katy clutched harder at her mum's hand.

"Please stay. Please. *Please*."

"I would if I could, angel, but it doesn't work that way."

"What doesn't?"

There was a long pause before Mum spoke. "Life."

"Why not?"

"It just doesn't."

"Did you go away because of me? Because of something I did?" asked Katy.

"Of course not. Never, ever think that," Mum's expression was almost fierce as she looked down at Katy. "You couldn't do anything to drive me away. Not one, single thing. Don't you realize that I love you? Don't you realise how much?"

"Then why did you go?"

"I didn't have any choice – I told you."

Katy looked out of the window. She couldn't see beyond it, because everything was swimmy and blurred. Mum placed gentle fingers beneath Katy's face, tilting it upwards, before she wiped away the tears trickling down Katy's cheeks.

"Can I come with you?" Katy whispered.

"Ah! I wondered if that was what you had in mind," said Mum, softly.

"Please let me come with you," Katy pleaded.

"Katy, I can't."

"Why?"

Mum considered for a moment. "Come with me. I've got something to show you," said Mum.

"What?"

"Come with me." Mum led the way across the bedroom to the door.

Katy suddenly felt nervous. "Can't we stay here?"

"Come on, love. There's nothing to be afraid of," smiled Mum.

And she opened the bedroom door.

Katy immediately pulled back. The cold and dark and shadows from the landing rushed in to meet them.

"This way," said Mum.

She led the way out of the bedroom to the top of the stairs. And with each step, Katy felt that, little by little, her blood was freezing in her veins. It was like walking into a nightmare. A nightmare that Katy knew. A nightmare that was on the edge of her mind and the tip of her tongue if she could just reach out and remember it. But she didn't want to. She didn't want to remember. She fought against it but the memory kept pushing at her. And with each step down the

stairs it got worse. Mum's hand around hers was the only warm thing that Katy had to cling on to. They were half way down the stairs when Katy heard the strange noises – sniffing and snuffling and sighing.

"No!"

Katy pulled away from Mum, turned and ran. She ran and ran back up to the warmth of her room, back to the safety of the known. Only when she was in her bed, did she turn to make sure Mum was behind her. But she wasn't. Mum was nowhere to be seen.

"Mum? Mum! Mum!" Katy called for her mum over and over. And each time she called, the darkness from the landing crept into the room and closer and closer towards her.

"Katy, wake up! Katy, wake up. It's just a bad dream."

Katy's eyes fluttered open to see Dad sitting at the edge of the bed, leaning over her.

"Dad? What're you doing here?"

"I heard you shouting. You were having a nightmare," Dad replied.

"No, I wasn't. I was with Mum. Where's Mum?" Katy looked around her room.

Dad shook his head. "Mum's not here any more, Katy. It was just a dream."

Katy's hands flew to her dreamcatcher, now lying at her side in the bed. A dream... No, it wasn't. It was more than just a dream. But Katy didn't know how to explain that, so she didn't even try. But she still had her dreamcatcher – and she still had two more nights to persuade Mum to either stay or take Katy with her.

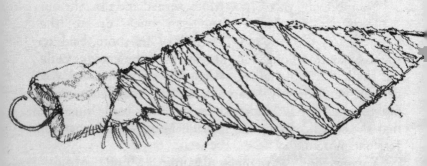

The following night, Katy went to sleep clasping her dreamcatcher and exactly the same thing happened. Mum appeared and they talked for a while by the window – and Katy had never been so happy. But all too soon Mum wanted to take Katy downstairs. They didn't spend as much time talking as the previous night.

"It's time to go downstairs," Mum said, softly.

"I don't want to," Katy pleaded as before.

But Mum insisted. Katy made it through the icy coldness which filled every part of the landing and the staircase, but as they crossed the hall to the living room, Katy's heart was pounding so hard, she thought it was going to explode within her. The sniffing, snuffling sounds were in there, louder than before.

"I can't!" Katy pulled away from Mum and ran all the way upstairs to the safety of her bedroom.

She threw herself on the bed and screamed and screamed

for Mum – but it was just another nightmare. Or so Dad said. He sat with her and stroked her hair until Katy closed her eyes. But when he left, Katy sobbed, her face against her pillow. She wept until, exhausted, she cried herself to sleep. Mum hadn't stayed and Katy only had one more night.

On the last night, Katy couldn't wait to go to sleep, but Dad didn't seem to want to leave the room.

"Are you sure you don't want me to stay with you, princess?" he asked.

"No, I'm fine Dad. Honest."

"No more nightmares – OK?"

"I promise," Katy forced a smile.

Dad headed off downstairs, leaving the bedroom door slightly ajar. Katy longed for her dream to come and take her, but she had trouble falling asleep. The slightest noise woke her up immediately. Katy clung to her dreamcatcher, praying and hoping and wishing to fall asleep properly so that she could dream. One night. That was all she needed. Just one more night.

"Katy, we don't have much time."

Mum took Katy by the hand and headed straight out of the room and down the stairs. They'd reached the closed living-room door before Katy could catch her breath.

"Open the door, darling," Mum urged.

"If I do, will you take me with you?" Katy said desperately.

"If you still want me to," said Mum.

Katy gathered all her courage to her like a flimsy cloak. Her hand crept through the darkness to the door.

"Katy…" Mum began, but then her voice faded to nothing.

Katy closed her eyes and opened the door. She could still hear the sniffing, snuffling sounds she'd heard the previous night. With frightened reluctance, she opened her eyes. She couldn't help it. Katy stood and stared. The room was lit by a single lamp and there on the sofa sat Dad, a photo album on his lap.

And he was crying.

Katy ran over to him. "Dad, what's the matter?"

And in that moment, the dream vanished. Katy was wide awake and she hated it – because being awake hurt her eyes and hurt her heart.

Startled, Dad looked up. "Katy what're you doing out of bed?"

"Why're you crying?" asked Katy. "Is it…is it because of Mum?"

Dad didn't answer. Fresh tears flowed down his face.

"Is it because…she isn't coming back?" asked Katy.

Dad nodded and held out his arms towards Katy. She scrambled up onto his lap and hugged him as tight as she could.

"I'm sorry, princess. I'm so sorry." Dad's tears mingled with Katy's as they hugged each other.

"Don't worry, Dad," whispered Katy. "Mum going away was just an accident. It wasn't your fault and it wasn't my fault either. And Mum would've stayed if she could. She told me so."

"I miss her so much," Dad admitted.

"So do I," whispered Katy.

"I don't know what I'd do if I lost you, too," said Dad. "I've tried to be strong for both of us, but every time it gets close to the anniversary of her death, I just crumble inside."

"We've still got each other," said Katy, tears still trickling down her cheeks.

Dad nodded. He couldn't have spoken if he wanted to. They sat together in the lamp light, hugging each other tightly in their shared grief. And in the doorway, the ghost of Katy's mum faded away. Katy and Dad were together again, a family again. Mum smiled sadly as she watched them. They were going to be all right. The dreamcatcher wasn't needed any more.

The World's Only English Comanche
Robert Swindells

Hello. My name's Florence and I want to tell you a story. It's about something that happened to me a very long time ago, when I was a little girl.

It was wartime, the second world war, and I was staying with my great aunt Laura in Tiverton. Mum and Dad lived in London, but the city was being bombed every night so they'd sent me to Devon where I'd be safe. Well I *was* safe, but I wasn't happy.

You see, this wasn't a holiday for me. I might be at my great aunt's for a long time, so I had to go to school, and that was the trouble. The children of Tiverton had never met anyone from London before. "Cor," one of them said, the first time I opened my mouth, "don't she *talk* queer?" It was in the playground, my first morning. Kids gathered round, poking me and laughing.

"*Say* something," they jeered, "go on, say *anything*." Mum had told me to be polite to everyone so I said, "Good morning, my name's Florence, what's yours?"

"Mickey Mouse," says one. "*Minnie* Mouse," says another. "Rumplestiltskin," says someone else. They're all laughing, pushing me round the ring.

After a minute the teacher came out. "What on *earth* is going on?" she snapped, barging into the middle. "It's like a bear garden out here. Oh," she said when she saw me, "you must be the girl from London. You haven't made a very good start here, have you Florence?"

It wasn't fair. *I* hadn't started it. I tried to tell her but she said, "Never mind that now, you'd better come to the cloakroom and tidy yourself: we're not used to slum dwellers in Tiverton."

That wasn't fair either. I *wasn't* a slum dweller. We had a nice house, in St. John's Wood, but the children heard her and from then on that was my nickname: Slum dweller. "Hey Slum dweller," somebody would yell across the playground, "how many rats d'you eat for breakfast?" And somebody else would holler, "She don't eat the *rats*, Maysie: the rats eats 'er."

It was no use telling the teacher. Miss Norton she was called and she hated me, I could tell. "Stop that chattering, Florence," she'd snap, when it was Maysie Malin or one of the other girls. She even blamed me if it was a *boy* talking. *And* she gave me all the dirty jobs. "Wash out the inkwells, Florence, and see you don't get ink under your nails."

It was no good telling great aunt Laura either. She was old. She'd forgotten how cruel children can be, and she wouldn't have a word said against Miss Norton. "Miss Norton is a fine teacher," she told me, "her mother taught *me*." And that was that.

The children chased me home every afternoon. One of the boys, Martin Perrigo, made up this chant:

Slum dweller, Slum dweller
Chucks her rubbish down the cellar.

It was stupid, didn't make sense, but it was upsetting to have it shouted after me along the lane every day. I took to shooting out of school ahead of everybody and taking the long way home across the fields, or else hiding in the lavatories till everybody had gone. Sometimes, when the children had been particularly mean to me, I'd creep into an old shed I found at the edge of somebody's field, think about Mum and Dad and have a good long cry.

One Friday afternoon at the end of a very bad week, I was huddled in a corner of the shed with my face in my hands, weeping like Scarlet O'Hara, when a shadow fell across me. I peeped through my fingers and saw a man looking down at me. He was silhouetted against the open door so I couldn't tell what he looked like, except he was in some sort of uniform. I wasn't scared, but I felt daft I'd been caught crying and I got up, rubbing my eyes with my knuckles.

"Hey, whatsamatter baby?" He sounded exactly like somebody in the pictures so I knew he was American. I felt even more embarrassed. "It...it's nothing," I croaked, "just, I don't come from around here and everybody laughs at me because they say I talk funny and the teacher, she..." Without warning an aching lump grew in my throat and I burst into floods of tears: couldn't help myself.

He put his arms around me and started sort of rocking me, as if I were a baby. "Hey come *on*," he crooned in my ear, "it can't be *that* bad surely: who looks after you?"

I managed to choke out great aunt Laura's name. He stroked my hair. "Well heck," he murmured, "I'm a long ways from home, too, and I wish I had a great aunt Laura looking out for *me*." He produced a big brown handkerchief. "Here: blow. Where's she live, your great aunt?"

He told me his name was Joe, asked what mine was, said he'd walk me home. Outside, I was surprised to see his skin was a reddish brown colour. He saw me looking, which was embarrassing, but he grinned. "Yup, I'm an Indian. Comanche. You know: like in the western movies?"

"Oh. I…didn't know there were still…" I broke off, blushing.

"Oh yeah, cowboys never managed to shoot *all* of us, Florence." He smiled. "See, I know just how you're feeling, 'cause people think *I* talk funny too, when I talk my own way. Listen." He rattled something off I couldn't make head nor tail of, then said, "I reckon your friends at school'd laugh at *that*, don't you?"

I shook my head. "They're not my friends."

"Well not right now maybe, but they'll come around, give 'em time to get used to you."

I nodded. "They *would* laugh, Joe. Is that Comanche you were talking?"

"Yup. So you see, we've a couple of things in common, you and me. We're both a long ways from home, we miss our moms and dads and we talk funny."

"Where's home for you, Joe?" I was surprised how easy I was finding it to call him by his first name. I mean, in those days children never called grown-ups by their first names, it was considered rude, but it didn't feel rude with Joe. I suppose that was because he was so natural with me, as if he were talking to an adult.

112

"Home?" He gazed into the sky with a wistful look. I felt as though we were in a film. "Home for me's Oklahoma. Big skies, wide open spaces. I'd be there now, 'cept the army wanted me special."

"Special? How?"

"*How.*" He said it deep, like a film Indian, then laughed. We were nearly at my great aunt's house but I didn't want our walk to end. This was the first time I'd been happy in Tiverton.

"Well I'll tell you, Florence, but you've gotta promise me you won't tell another living soul, 'cause this is top secret." He held my arm. We stopped. He looked into my eyes. "I'm not kidding now, *top secret.* I'm telling you 'cause...well, 'cause we funny talkers gotta stick together, right? But if you tell anybody *any part* of what I'm gonna tell you now I'll be shot, you'll go to jail and the crazy white man'll win the war."

"Crazy white man?"

"Yeah, that's Comanche for Hitler." He gazed at me. "Can I trust you, Florence?"

I nodded. "Yes."

"With my life: with a whole *lot* of lives?"

"I promise."

"OK, sit yourself down on this bit of wall and listen." I sat, he stood in front of me and started speaking in a low voice and this is what he told me.

"In war, fighting men have to send messages to one another by radio. Trouble is, the enemy listens in. He intercepts the messages, then he knows what we're going to do before we do it. He's there waiting for us, and we walk right into his ambush. Now to prevent this, people invent all sorts of clever codes so the enemy won't know what we're saying, but no matter how clever the code, sooner or later the enemy cracks it. There's no such thing as an uncrackable code. And that's where I come in: me and my pals."

"How d'you mean?"

"Me and my buddies, we're all Comanches. We talk Comanche." He smiled. "No German talks Comanche. No German understands it. Comanche has never been written down. There are no Comanche books. No Comanche dictionary. We *talk* Comanche, we don't write it. There's no such thing as Comanche writing. So, when my commander wants to send a message and keep it secret from the enemy, he whispers it to me in English, I radio it to my buddy in Comanche, he whispers it to his commander in English and there you are: if the enemy's been listening, all he's heard is a lot of Indian talk he can't begin to understand. It's the only uncrackable code."

I was flabbergasted by the cleverness of the idea, *and* because Joe entrusted his dangerous secret to me. I'd never tell of course. Never never, and I think he knew that. He smiled down at me in the dusk of early May. "So you see Florence: there's more to us funny talkers than most people realize. To the rest of the army, my pals and me're just a bunch of no-good Injuns, and we have to let 'em go on thinking that 'cause the truth, the *real* truth, is a secret. And now you're one of us: one of the funny talkers that'll help win this war, and the world's only English Comanche." He winked. "You remember that, next time those poor dopes're laughing at you. Remember it *every* time."

And that's it. That's my story. He walked me over to my aunt's gate, said goodnight and strolled off down the lane and out of my life. We never met again, but everything had changed because of him. Oh, the children still chased me home and Miss Norton didn't get to like me any better, but I didn't care. In June the allied armies landed in occupied France and I knew Joe was there somewhere, talking funny. By September there was no more danger in London so Dad came and took me home, and the following spring the war ended.

From time to time over the years I wondered what happened to Joe. Did he survive the war, go home to Oklahoma? I hoped so, but assumed I'd never know.

Then the other night I saw my Comanche on TV. He was in France, being presented with a medal for what he did there more than fifty years ago. He looked really old but then he would: I'm growing old myself.

Still talk funny as well. And still the world's only English Comanche.

Fat Harry
Jeremy Strong

The other children called him Pogo, so he called his sister Pottyfilla and his hamster Fat Harry. Pogo was not, of course, his real name, which was Ryan Schick. Ryan was lanky. He stood several centimetres above everyone else in his class. His full nickname was Pogo Stick. Ryan didn't like his nickname, but then who does? No, he didn't like his nickname, so he gave nicknames to everything around him. Even his hamster.

Fat Harry was not particularly fat. He just looked fat, because his fur was thick and fluffy, especially when Ryan back-combed it. Fat Harry was white all over, except for one black paw on his rear left leg, and a single black patch slap-bang on top of his right eye.

The hamster lived in Ryan's bedroom. He had one of those multi-purpose cages – a kind of hamster playpen. It had tunnels and hiding places and several different levels to clamber about on and, of course, it had a wheel. How Harry loved that wheel! He would climb inside and get things rolling. Within seconds the wheel would be humming so fast you couldn't see the spokes. All you could hear was the rotating rumble and all you could see was Fat Harry, his upper body hardly moving, his legs a blur.

Every evening Ryan would take Fat Harry out of his playpen. Ryan would lie on his bed and let Harry run around. The hamster would sit on Ryan's open hand, nose twitching, and Ryan would tell Harry everything. In fact, the hamster probably knew more about Ryan than anyone else in the world, except Ryan, of course.

Ryan would lie there, whispering into the hamster's tiny pink ears. "You remember I told you about Sophie, in our class? She likes Darren. Darren! She must be crazy! He's got a face like a pig-bin. I got into trouble today. I forgot to learn my spellings. Aren't words weird? Why do you have to spell 'because' like that? I'd spell it 'becos'. Well, I did spell it 'becos' so I got it wrong. Words are stupid. Darren's stupid. Sophie must be stupid if she likes him. Do you think you can be beautiful and stupid? That's not fair, is it? Darren says he's going to take Sophie on the London Eye and he's going to kiss her when they get to the top. Well, I hope he falls off! Anyhow, I'm saving up my pocket money. You mustn't tell anyone, it's a secret, I'm saving it so that I can get plastic surgery. Yeah! I'm going to have plastic surgery and I shall come out looking like a film star and Sophie will swoon at my feet and say, 'My hero! Will you marry me?' and I shall say, 'Yes, my darling!' and she'll kiss me. Darren will be green with envy and he'll probably go off and become a monk or live on a remote island all by himself for the rest of his life, sobbing his heart out."

Fat Harry would sit on Ryan's hand and listen to him rambling on. It was a good thing that Fat Harry was a good listener because Ryan had a lot of secrets to tell him. Who else was there to tell? Ryan could hardly tell his Mum such things. As for Pottyfilla (real name Jade), she was much too young.

When Ryan finished talking, he would put Fat Harry back in his playpen. As the evening went on, the hamster would become more lively. Hamsters are generally nocturnal creatures, so Harry would wake up just as Ryan was going to sleep. Ryan would drift into dreamland to the merry whirring of the hamster wheel.

You could say that Fat Harry and Ryan were great buddies – if you can be friends with a hamster. Harry needed Ryan to provide him with food and shelter. Ryan needed Harry to provide him with comfort (and his little pink ears, full of secrets).

Everything was fine until the day Fat Harry became seriously ill.

The hamster lay on the floor of his cage, hardly moving. Ryan could just about make out the hollow rise and fall of Harry's chest as he struggled to breathe. He seized the whole playpen and stumbled downstairs with it.

"Mum! Look! Harry's ill! Do something!"

Mrs Schick put Harry and Ryan and Jade in the back of the car and they set off for the vet's surgery. It was a terrible day to be out anywhere. Rain was falling out of the sky as if a gigantic bath was overflowing. Great slashes of lightning stabbed the gloom over and over again. Thunder crashed around the little car as it swished and splashed and sloshed its way to the surgery. By the time they had parked, got out of the car and rushed indoors they were soaking.

"Quick! Quick!" cried Ryan. "Fat Harry is dying!"

The hamster was rushed straight to the vet, Mr Carmichael. He examined Harry carefully. The little creature lay on his side, barely breathing. Mr Carmichael bent over Harry and listened to the hamster with his stethoscope.

"What's the matter with him?" whispered Ryan.

"It's his heart," declared the vet.

"Will he be all right?"

The windows rattled as another outburst of thunder went drumming across the sky, and rain lashed the glass. The vet looked dubious.

"It's…difficult to say. Hamsters don't always live very long. Their hearts beat so fast – they wear out quickly."

"I've got money saved," said Ryan. "If I pay, can you give him a heart swap?"

Mr Carmichael smiled and shook his head. "We can't do that kind of surgery on a hamster," he explained. "I'm sorry."

"There must be something you can do!" cried Ryan. "You can't let him die!"

Jade began struggling in Mrs Schick's arms.

"Potty," she said, in a sing-song voice that got louder and louder. "Potty, potty, potty, POTTY, PITTY-POTTY, MUMMY!"

"Oh dear," said Mrs Schick. "I'm sorry, is there a toilet we can use?"

The vet pointed the way and Mrs Schick went off, saying she'd be back very shortly. More lightning flashed and the lights in the vet's surgery flickered and then came back on.

Ryan stared at Mr Carmichael and the vet shook his head.

"I'm sorry. Hamsters have weak…" his voice trailed away. He couldn't bear to see the look on Ryan's face. "There is one thing we can try. I don't think it's ever been used on a hamster, but we could try, I suppose. It's our only chance. I have a machine I sometimes use to help get an animal's heart going if it stops. We don't use it on creatures as small as hamsters, but we'll have a go. I shall turn down the electric current. There. Now we power up. Stand back."

The vet held two electrodes to the hamster's furry chest. "And go!" At the exact moment that the machine was supposed to deliver a tiny shock to Fat Harry's heart, a bolt of lightning struck the surgery.

FIZZANGGG!

For a few moments Ryan thought that the world was going to end. Everything around him took on an unearthly glow. Sparks fizzed and spluttered around the surgery, leaping and jumping from one object to another. The lights went out completely and the air seemed to hum and crackle. On the table, Harry lay in an eerie cocoon of dancing blue squiggles of electric current.

Slowly a kind of normality returned. Mr Carmichael and Ryan stood like statues, gazing around, wondering what had happened. The only movement in the room came from the examination table, where a small creature was running about, sniffing eagerly at strange smells.

"Harry! You're OK!" cried Ryan, as if he had woken from a dream.

"Good heavens," murmured the vet. "The little thing's all right. Who would have believed it?"

At that moment, Mrs Schick came back with the baby. "There was the most awful bang. The lights went out. I thought the world had ended. Oh my! Is that Harry? He's better! What a clever vet you are!"

And so they took Fat Harry home.

In fact, Fat Harry had never been so well in all his life. He even put on a growing spurt. "You really will be Fat Harry if you get any fatter," laughed Ryan.

"He seems to get bigger every day," Mrs Schick said.

"Me big," squeaked Jade, before squeezing up her face and making a rather revolting noise and an even more revolting smell. "Potty Mummy!"

Ryan groaned. "You're supposed to ask for your potty before you go to the loo, Jade, not after."

Mrs Schick was still gazing at Fat Harry. "He really is a very large hamster," she murmured. She gathered up Jade and set off to change her.

That night, Ryan lay on his bed and whispered into Fat Harry's ears. "I think I might write a letter to Sophie. I can't talk to her. I try to, but the words vanish from my head and I don't know what to say. Anyhow, that Darren is nearly always hanging around her. He's like a bad smell. He's worse than Pottyfilla! Do you think Sophie will go out with me? She's got a really nice smile, don't you think? Oh no, you've never seen her. Well, I think she's amazing. Mum's right. You have grown.

You only used to fill half my hand, and now I can't see my palm at all. And you weigh more, too."

Ryan put the hamster back in the playpen and settled down to sleep. Fat Harry just about managed to squeeze back into his wheel. It began to spin. The axle squeaked and scraped and then all at once the whole thing collapsed. Fat Harry scrambled out from the wreckage.

Ryan sat up and switched on the light. "Oh Harry! You've broken your wheel. You're too heavy, you big fat lump. Now go and lie down or something. I'm tired."

Ryan put out the light and went back to sleep. Fat Harry sat in the corner of his cage and did a bit more growing. He grew so much that he was able to reach up to the top of his cage and push the lid to one side. He scrambled out and moments later he was standing on Ryan's desk. He grew some more. Then some more. And more still.

When morning came Fat Harry was the size of a small cat. He had curled up on the end of Ryan's bed and was fast asleep.

Ryan could not believe his eyes. He picked up Fat Harry and carried the hamster through to his mother. "Look," he said, shaking her awake.

Mrs Schick was as astonished as Ryan. She stroked Harry's thick fur and shook her head. "I have never seen such a big hamster," she murmured. "There is something strange going on here."

And she was right. By the time breakfast was over Fat Harry was as big as a sheepdog. Ryan put him on an old dog lead and took him to school, where everyone was astonished. Darren tried not to be impressed, and he just laughed. "That's not a hamster!" he sniggered, "it's an elephamster!"

"Ha ha," muttered Ryan.

"He's lovely," cooed Sophie, "can I hold his lead?"

"Yes, but I shall have to hold your other hand."

"Why?"

"Because Fat Harry is very strong and I don't want him to pull you over and hurt you."

"You're so sweet," Sophie blushed, and Ryan thought she looked even prettier than normal. Darren pushed forward angrily. "Ryan's just trying it on with you," he protested, but it was no use. Sophie gave him a scathing glance.

"When you've got a big hamster like Ryan I might want to speak to you," she said. "Besides, you said you'd take me on the London Eye, and you didn't."

"It's broken!" cried Darren. "It's not my fault it stopped," but Sophie had turned her back on him.

Ryan thought this was wonderful, but his delight did not last very long. The trouble was that Fat Harry was getting bigger – and BIGGER! By the end of the school day the hamster was as large as an Alsatian and it wasn't fun any longer – it was worrying.

Mrs Schick told Ryan to leave Harry out in the garden overnight. "If you bring him indoors and he carries on growing at that speed he'll knock the house down." So Ryan left Harry outside and by morning the hamster had gone. Ryan rushed outside but he need not have worried. Fat Harry was across the road in the park, eating all the flowers and

bushes and the smaller trees. Now the hamster was as big as a horse, and he was still growing. Panic set in. The police took over. They wouldn't let anyone near the beast in case Harry attacked them. Even Ryan was told to keep away, and Sophie stopped speaking to him because she said she didn't like boys with monsters.

"Darren's got a goldfish," she said. "And it's very small and it stays the same size. It can blow bubbles, too."

"I bet your elephamster can't blow bubbles," sneered Darren.

"He could if he was underwater," Ryan pointed out.

"He'd drown," sniggered Darren. "You're stupid."

He took Sophie's hand and off they went. Ryan watched them miserably. So much for that little romance, he thought. You just can't trust girls.

The police tried to catch the creature but Harry was too big, or too quick or too clever. Nobody could get near him. The police asked the fire brigade to help, but they just made everything and everyone wet. By this time Harry really was as big as an elephant. The fire brigade asked the army to help and soon tanks were rolling out of the army barracks and off on Fat Harry's trail. They had orders to shoot Harry when they saw him.

"That hamster is a danger to the public," said the Prime Minister on the television news that night.

"That's ridiculous," shouted Ryan. "Fat Harry would not hurt a fly!" But nobody listened to him. Ryan couldn't bear it, and he couldn't sleep either.

He knew he had to do something. He got out of bed and slipped on his clothes. Then he set off in the dark night to search for his pet hamster.

It was strange and eerie to be out on the streets at night. The police had told everyone to stay indoors because there was a giant hamster on the loose. Even half the police were so scared that they stayed at home with the bed covers pulled over their heads. The only movement came from the odd tank as it rumbled past, searching for the escaped monster.

126

It was early morning before Ryan spotted the hamster. Fat Harry was down by the River Thames, eating trees along The Embankment. Unfortunately, the army had seen the hamster, too, and were moving their tanks into position.

Ryan ran forward, just as the army were taking aim with their big guns. "Stop!" he yelled. "Fat Harry won't do any harm!"

And it was at that moment that Ryan had his bright idea. He turned to Fat Harry and spoke so quietly that Harry had to put his gigantic head down close to the ground, so that Ryan could whisper into his huge, pink ear. Ryan smiled and turned back towards the Prime Minister.

"Just watch this!" he cried. He lead Harry along the side of the river until they reached the London Eye, which was standing still and broken. Fat Harry climbed inside the giant wheel and began to walk. The wheel began to turn slowly, then a little faster, then faster still.

"The wheel is working!" everyone shouted. "Look! Fat Harry is making the wheel work! That's amazing! What a brilliant, clever hamster he is!"

And that is how things are to this day. Fat Harry makes the wheel go round and everyone can ride on it. The very first person to go on the wheel was Ryan Schick. And guess who he took with him? No, not Sophie. He took Lucy instead. Lucy wasn't as pretty as Sophie, but she was much, much nicer, and she kissed him when they got to the top.

There was one other thing, too. Everyone at Ryan's school suddenly stopped calling him Pogo Stick. After all, you'd be daft to give nicknames to someone with a giant hamster. But Ryan still calls his sister Pottyfilla.

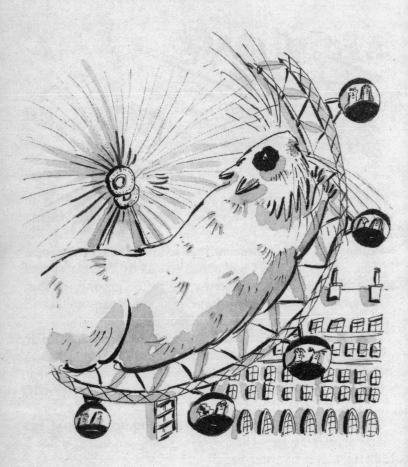